"I'm taking my son, Penny. None of you can stop me," Jake said.

Her son's father—the FBI's most wanted right now—fired another round of shots, causing Zeke to rush toward Penny and push her down, his body shielding hers.

"Why did you let him go?" Penny screamed at Zeke. She struggled to get up. But Zeke was still blocking her, protecting her. Then she stared into his chocolate eyes.

Something swift and sizzling moved between them in a flash of emotion.

"I had to for now," Zeke replied as he placed his hands on either side of her shoulders and shot up. Helping her to her feet, he added, "I know my brother. He'd shoot you and Cheetah or he'd ambush us later. He wants you dead so he can take my nephew."

"*Your* nephew?"

"Yes," he replied, defiance in his eyes. "Kevin is your son—*and* my nephew. I have to get to him before Jake does."

* * *

CLASSIFIED K-9 UNIT:
These lawmen solve the toughest cases
with the help of their brave canine partners

With over seventy books published and millions in print, **Lenora Worth** writes award-winning romance and romantic suspense. Three of her books finaled in the ACFW Carol Awards, and her Love Inspired Suspense novel *Body of Evidence* became a *New York Times* bestseller. Her novella in *Mistletoe Kisses* made her a *USA TODAY* bestselling author. Lenora goes on adventures with her retired husband, Don, and enjoys reading, baking and shopping...especially shoe shopping.

Visit the Author Profile page at Harlequin.com for more titles.

TRACKER

LENORA WORTH

HARLEQUIN® LOVE INSPIRED® SUSPENSE

Special thanks and acknowledgment are given to Lenora Worth for her contribution to the Classified K-9 Unit miniseries.

Recycling programs
for this product may
not exist in your area.

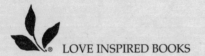

® LOVE INSPIRED BOOKS

ISBN-13: 978-0-373-67845-7

Tracker

www.Harlequin.com

Printed in U.S.A.

Through the praise of children and infants you have established a stronghold against your enemies, to silence the foe and the avenger.
—*Psalms* 8:2

To the other authors in this series who always help me, brainstorm with me and laugh with me—Terri Reed, Valerie Hansen, Lynette Eason, Laura Scott and Shirlee McCoy. I love working with all of you! And to my editor, Emily Rodmell, for putting up with me!

ONE

"I'm not leaving without my son."

He pressed the gun against her spine, the cold muzzle chilling against her thin shirt. Late-afternoon sunshine shot over the Elk Basin, giving the vast Montana sky a pastoral rendering. But right now, that sky looked ominous.

She didn't want to die here.

Penny Potter twisted around and tried to break free from the man who'd come crashing out of the woods and tackled her just seconds before. Heaving a shuddering breath, she screamed at her former boyfriend, "Jake, there is no way I'm letting you take Kevin out of the country! I told you last time, neither of us is going with you."

Jake Morrow's blue eyes matched the sky, but the bitter flash of anger seared Penny's heart. "Yeah, but you took my boy and ran away."

Apprehension and fear gnawed at her, but

Penny tried to stay calm. She had to keep her head and get back to Kevin before her ex found him. "I can't leave the country with you. I'm not going to put Kevin through that. They're all looking for you, Jake. Just go and leave us alone."

"*You* might not be willing to come with me," Jake said, his actions filled with a wild recklessness that made her shiver in spite of the late summer heat. "But my son sure is not staying behind. You're going to take me to him. Now! Or you'll never see him again."

Special Agent Zeke Morrow moved silently through the underbrush, his K-9 partner, an Australian shepherd named Cheetah, taking the lead as they canvassed yet another grid of rocky hills and tall ponderosa pines. He'd checked in with several of the other members of the FBI Classified K-9 Unit who were scouring a ridge on the other side of the woods. Nothing yet. No sign of Jake Morrow.

"Where are you, Jake?" he asked in a low whisper, his gaze scanning every shift of leaves and every snap of twigs. He had to keep going in spite of the deep-boned fatigue that threatened to weigh him down.

Could his half brother, Jake, really be somewhere inside this vast wilderness? After picking up a tip that the former agent, now wanted by the FBI for turning corrupt and joining forces with the infamous Dupree crime syndicate, had been spotted buying supplies and ammunition at a truck stop a few miles from here, Zeke had talked to several of the residents who lived along the edge of the wilderness preserve. One of them, a young science teacher who'd been on a hike, had seen someone matching Jake's description going into the Elk Basin early this morning.

"And there was another man with him but he took off in a big black van," the nervous fellow had stated. "Don't mention my name, okay? Those two looked loaded for bear."

The other guy had been described as short in stature with long, stringy hair and wearing glasses. Sounded a lot like Gunther Caprice, a wanted criminal who'd managed to fly under the radar since the Dupree family business had started to unravel. He'd probably dropped Jake off here and was hiding out somewhere. But what were they doing here of all places?

Unless this was another one of his brother's ruses to fool all of them. Or…perhaps this was the big break they'd all been waiting for.

Zeke's gut told him that his half brother was indeed somewhere in these woods. But that still didn't explain why Jake had decided to come back to Montana when he knew he was a wanted man. What possible motive could he have?

Jake, who'd once been a valuable member of the elite FBI Classified K-9 Unit, had gone off the deep end after joining up with the notorious Dupree crime family. Fellow agent Ian Slade had fallen in love with the only crime-free member of the Dupree clan. Esme Dupree was willing to testify against her brother, Reginald, but she'd left the witness protection program because she feared for her life. Ian grudgingly became her protector after a trek through the Florida Everglades, where eventually her older sister, Violetta, shot and killed Angus Dupree in order to save Esme's life. But now Ian and Esme had gone into hiding in another country until Jake was found and Reginald Dupree was brought to justice. Couldn't happen soon enough for Zeke. The whole team had been playing a game of cat and mouse with Jake all spring and summer.

Almost six months of searching for his armed and dangerous half brother had brought Zeke back to Montana a couple of days ago. Reports kept coming in—sightings of the rogue agent near the Elk Basin and in other areas close to Billings. Was he trying to get back to headquarters? Or was Jake just messing with the entire team?

I have to find him and try to reason with him, take him in alive.

Zeke stopped and gave Cheetah some water, patted him and checked the dog's protective FBI vest. "Good boy. You're doing great. Show me where to go next, okay?"

Cheetah would do his job. The medium-sized dog had a sweet temperament, but he was trained in search and rescue and could turn serious with one command. His K-9 partner never quit, so Zeke wouldn't, either.

Cheetah lifted his snout and sniffed the hot August air. Then the dog tugged at his leash and headed east, back toward the main trail out of the basin.

Zeke followed, the sound of distant voices causing his pulse to rise. Could he finally be on the right track?

"No!" Penny tried to break away, but Jake grabbed her by the collar of her shirt and jerked her back so hard pain shot through her neck. Praying her son was okay, she tried to stay calm so she could see a way out of this.

Shoving her ahead of him on the rocky path into the thicket, Jake kept one hand in a death grip on her arm. "Let's go. We're getting Kevin, and either you both go with me, or I'll take him and you won't even have time to regret it."

"You don't have to do this," she pleaded, wondering how Jake had found her. She'd been all over the country, using fake names, constantly changing her appearance and hiding out in dives with her now two-year-old son. Penny hated dragging Kevin from pillar to post and hiding him in secrecy, but she had to protect him from his father. She'd thought since almost six months had passed and no one had found Jake, she'd be safe coming back to Montana. Especially here in the remote wilderness in the Elk Basin, an area she'd loved all of her life.

But then, she'd always underestimated the dangerous man holding her against her will now. Penny had wanted to believe Jake was one of the good guys, but she could tell even before he'd disappeared that he'd changed. She'd heard the rumors and a few cryptic news reports after he'd been presumed kidnapped by a member of the Dupree crime family. But as the months wore on, things had taken a sickening twist.

Now Jake was wanted by the very people who used to trust him and work with him—his own FBI team. Their work was classified, but she knew they'd searched her former house and probably taken some pictures she'd left there so they could easily identify her and Kevin. They were most likely searching for her, too. She'd taken off long before they showed up, and she'd had to leave several other temporary locations.

All because she'd been trying to get away from Jake.

Her ex was in deep trouble and from what she could glean, it had something to do with the criminal syndicate that his former unit had tried to infiltrate several months ago. Jake had gone missing once the dust had settled on that botched mission. She'd heard they'd captured Reginald Dupree that day, but his uncle Angus Dupree had escaped and taken Jake hostage. Angus was dead now, or so she'd heard. All she knew was Jake was a wanted man, according to the few news reports she'd heard.

The reports had also implicated Jake as a willing accomplice. He'd betrayed his unit for money and power. And yet here he stood, holding a gun on her in a desperate attempt to get out of the country. With their son. That would happen over her dead body.

"Jake, let me go. You can't take a toddler on the run. Let us be and…maybe one day I can send you pictures or…find a way for you two to reunite."

"No," he barked. "No, Penny. I lost my father. I won't let that happen to my son."

Her heart sank. Jake was in a mindset where he refused to listen to reason. "I understand," she said, not giving up but giving in for now.

It was too late for Jake to do anything but run. He would kill her and take their son. He wouldn't give up without a fight, but neither would she.

Zeke's phone buzzed. "What's the status, Agent Morrow?"

Max West, the Special Agent in Charge, checking on him again.

"Cheetah's picked up something, sir. I heard voices on the other side of one of the main trails heading east. Headed that way now."

"I'll send some backup. We got nothing here."

After ending the call, Zeke put his phone away and listened. There. Again. Shouts into the still, dry air. A woman's scream.

Cheetah growled low and alerted. Zeke's heart pumped new energy into his tired body. They hurried through the scrub brush and outcroppings, but he couldn't decide if he was relieved or if this dread burdening his soul would overtake him.

Help me make the right decisions, Lord.

* * *

Jake clamped a sweaty hand over her mouth. "That was a big mistake," he said, his tone full of rage. "But I doubt anyone heard you. You're so predictable, Penny, hanging around out in the woods with people trying to have a wilderness adventure. I've been watching you for days, getting a handle on your routine. No one will ever find you out here." He dropped his hand. "But if you scream again, you'll regret it."

He was right.

Penny blinked away tears of frustration and looked around frantically at the deserted trail. No one in sight. She'd finished guiding a wilderness tour over an hour ago and watched the busload of about twenty people head out in the other direction. Tired and hot and not as alert as she should have been, she'd started hiking the couple of miles toward home, her mind on seeing Kevin. Jake had waylaid her near the small town of Iris Rock, where her son was safe inside the Wild Iris Inn with the owner, Claire Crayton.

Claire knew what to do. Penny had explained when she first moved into the boardinghouse that her ex-boyfriend might show up and try to cause trouble. Under no circumstance was the older woman to allow Kevin to go with anyone except Penny. Claire had nodded toward the shotgun she kept behind the check-in counter and promised her she'd take care of Kevin, no matter what.

Now Penny wished she'd warned Claire that the father of her child might be armed and dangerous and wanted by the law. But she'd never dreamed Jake would hold a gun on her or threaten her life.

Please, God, keep Kevin safe.

Penny entreated that simple prayer over and over while she looked around for a way to escape. Since she'd been a trained guide for years, she knew this basin better than most. She knew the nooks and crannies, the hills, valleys and meadows and all the streams and waterfalls; knew the animals and the seasons. If she could make it across the trailhead to the open meadow, she'd be able to hide in the tall grass and inch her way toward the foothills.

"Don't even think about it, sweetheart," Jake said, his breath hissing like a snake against her neck. "You're smart and I have no doubt that you can survive out here. But it would be stupid to try and outrun me."

Penny glanced at the semiautomatic handgun he pressed into her ribs as a reminder, her heart pumping adrenaline while she thought of her sweet little boy. Kevin had his daddy's dark blond hair and deep blue eyes.

"What happened to you, Jake?" she asked, stalling but also wanting some answers. "Why would you risk everything and ruin your career? I've heard rumors—"

"Later," he snarled. "I'm not going to explain all of that right now. Besides, what do you care? You ran out on me."

Pushing her forward, his anger shimmering from every pore, he checked both ways along the path into the woods.

He wasn't going to talk, and he was too wired to tolerate her feeble attempts to save herself. Penny cast a desperate glance over the vast open country between the surrounding hills, the August heat burning her. Her only chance was to try to run as fast as she possibly could. She waited for Jake to loosen his grip on her arm before she broke free and plowed through the brush, only to stumble on a jutting rock and fall face-first into the dry bramble.

He caught up with her and jerked her back up. "Nice try." Stroking a gentle finger against her cheekbone, he said, "Now you're bleeding. Next time, things might get even worse."

Zeke followed the sound of voices, Cheetah taking him back into the woods. A woman. A scream. Even if this didn't involve Jake, someone could be in trouble. Not many people hung around here this late unless they were camping or had gotten lost on one of the many trails. The sun would be setting in about an hour. Needing to think this through, he halted Cheetah to get his bearings and hurriedly checked the map coordinates on his phone. They were about two miles from the small town of Iris Rock.

The town where Penny Potter used to rent a house.

Penny had been Jake's girlfriend and she was now the mother of his child. But she was so off the radar, no one had been able to find her. Could Jake have come back here looking for her and his son, one last time? While that didn't make much sense, Zeke's gut burned with the sure knowledge that someone was in trouble up ahead.

"Let's go," he said to Cheetah. The animal took off in an eager run, straight toward those echoing voices.

Then Zeke heard something else off in the distance. The hum of a vehicle hitting ruts in the dirt. Hopefully, his backup had arrived.

"We'll keep walking," Jake explained. "I have someone coming with a vehicle full of supplies to pick us up just over that north ridge. We'll have our son and we can leave tonight. I have plenty of money hidden away, baby. We can go somewhere warm and tropical, a place where they will never find us. I'll take care of both of you." His husky whispers sent a cold chill down her spine. "I've missed you so much."

Now he was trying to sweet-talk her? Penny closed her eyes and swallowed back the painful knot lodged inside her throat. Resolve and revulsion overtook any sympathy she might have once had for him. She was strong now, strong in her newfound faith and strong in her love for her child. "I'm not going anywhere with you, Jake, and neither is Kevin."

"He's *my* son."

The words held a threat.

She had to make a move.

Penny practiced self-defense on a regular basis since her job required her to be out in the middle of nowhere with strangers following her around and wild animals approaching unexpectedly. But could she take down a six-foot-three-inch muscular man? A deranged, desperate fugitive who didn't have anything to lose?

Except the one person he loved in the world. His son.

Her heart swelled when she thought about Kevin. So innocent and precious. He'd never know his father. But if she didn't make a move, he'd never have his mother, either.

"Quit stalling, Penny," Jake said, his voice as hard and dry as the surrounding countryside. She stared at the flat, brown land leading to the distant woods and hills and spotted a lone scarlet-colored fairy trumpet. The pretty flower beckoned her. It had survived the hot summer. She would, too.

Lord, help me in my time of need. Give me the strength to do what I need to do.

With a grunt and all the energy she could muster, she whirled and elbowed Jake in the ribs, one booted foot latching against his left calf so she could trip him. Still in motion, she jabbed at his eyes with two fingers, surprising him.

He put a hand to his face and went down with a groan, giving her just enough time to slip out of his grip and slam her heavy backpack against his head.

Clutching the bag against her as protection, she spun away from his crumbled body and took off toward the forest about fifty yards across the meadow. If she could make it to the tree line, she could hide up in the hills until nightfall. Or longer if necessary. But she couldn't hide. She had to call the boardinghouse and warn Claire before Jake got to Kevin.

But right now she had to outrun the man she once loved. Her heart hammering in her chest, she pushed with all her might and took off, her hiking boots kicking up dust.

Thinking she'd made it, Penny glanced back when she was about ten yards from the thick stand of ponderosa pines and aspens leading to another trail. Jake stumbled toward her, his gun raised.

He wasn't going to let her live.

TWO

A gunshot echoed through the meadow just beyond the woods.

Zeke started running.

"Search," he commanded, letting Cheetah's leash go. The dog took off toward the area where they'd heard the shots, Zeke jogging behind him. Cheetah must have picked up some kind of scent that he recognized. But had it come from the same vicinity as that gunshot?

The showdown that Zeke had been waiting for for close to six months could be about to happen. And none too soon. Roaming all over the country trying to track down leads, desperately trying to rescue his older half brother, only to discover that the man he'd always worshipped had turned traitor, had taken its toll on him and the entire team. He'd even taken a bullet recently and still had the sore spot on his upper left arm to prove it. Thanks to his brother, he'd have a nice scar as a permanent reminder.

But nothing was going to stop Zeke from trying to track down Jake. Maybe he could at least keep him alive and in prison instead of dead and gone. If Jake was willing to give them vital information that could finish off the last dregs of the Dupree syndicate, maybe they could work out a plea bargain at least.

"Find him, Cheetah," Zeke said, the urgency of their situation driving him on.

Cheetah had Jake's scent from an old T-shirt they'd found in his locker back at headquarters in Billings, but they'd also confirmed the blood on a shirt they'd found in a cabin in Texas belonged to his brother, too. That, along with a watch Zeke had given him when Jake had first become an FBI agent. Zeke asked to be on the case and he'd followed the tips all over the country, hoping to end this thing. Now it could all end right here in Montana.

Zeke had images of his brawny half brother serving as a dedicated FBI Classified K-9 agent, now turned outright criminal, to spur him on. Yet, despite everything, he didn't want to accept that Jake was all bad. He had called Zeke not long ago and told him he was in too deep now. Just another reminder of how confusing things had become.

Hot and exhausted, both he and Cheetah hurried out of the thicket. Cheetah's low growl and urgent trot told Zeke he'd probably find his brother.

But had Jake been shot?

When they made it out into the open, Zeke sucked in a sharp breath. He couldn't believe what he was witnessing.

Jake had a woman held at gunpoint.

A woman who looked familiar based on the pictures he'd seen. And scared. She was bleeding, her left cheekbone bruised and swollen. Her gaze slammed into Zeke's and he felt a jolt of adrenaline rushing over him.

Penny Potter? It had to be her.

Zeke didn't hesitate. He needed to end this now.

"Drop the weapon," he ordered, his assault rifle aimed at Jake and the woman. Penny was the mother of Jake's young son, Kevin. Her golden-brown hair and slim, athletic figure sure fit the description. Her hair was shorter and heavily streaked with lighter shades of blond, but he remembered her face from some old photos they'd found when they'd searched her last known address in Colorado. The K-9 team had been looking for her since late spring but she'd managed to elude them, too. Zeke never imagined he'd find her here again and with Jake holding her hostage.

"It's over, Jake," he called, his gaze trained on his brother. "Don't make it any harder."

Jake didn't even flinch. Shoving the gun closer to the woman's stomach, he shouted, "Hello there, bro. Long time, no see." Then he shook his head and chuckled. "They had to send you, right?" Jake's dark blue gaze slid over Zeke's tactical uniform with disdain. "All geared up and loaded down to come after me. Poetic justice and so much irony, don't you think?"

Zeke advanced a little closer. Cheetah was silent but waiting for his command with a controlled tremor. "Jake, Cheetah can take you down but I don't want to force that. Put the weapon down and let the woman go. We can find a way to help you. Maybe work out a plea bargain or something."

He almost added a *please*, but Jake used to tease him about being weak-kneed and impulsive. Zeke couldn't show any weakness now, and he wasn't about to make any impulsive decisions. A woman's life depended on it. And the life of her child, too, if he was guessing right on her identity.

Jake shook his head and jammed the gun against the woman's ribs so hard, she cried out. But she quickly recovered, a determined grit in her expression. "It's not over until I have my son safely out of this country," he informed them. "I need to get Kevin. I'll be out of everyone's hair soon."

"You can't do that," Zeke said. "You don't want to take your son away from his mother."

Jake's gaze scanned the woods and trails. "What's left for me to do except leave? The Dupree family is shattered and their lieutenants are scattered to the wind. I'm on my own and…there's really no other way. I just want my son, so I'm going to get him. *Now.*"

He gripped Penny's arm and pushed her forward.

"I can't let you go," Zeke said, wondering if he'd have the courage to shoot his own half brother. Jake's desperate statement only made things worse. Turning his attention to the frightened woman, he asked, "Penny, are you okay?"

She gasped and nodded, her eyes filling with both relief and dread. Zeke could see the resolve in her gaze, too.

"She's fine," Jake gritted out, anger echoing in each word. "Turn around, Zeke. Let me get to my boy. I won't hurt her, I promise." Then he added, "And I don't want to shoot you again."

"I don't trust your promises," Zeke said. "I'm going to ask you one more time to drop your weapon."

With an angry grunt, Jake pulled Penny closer. "You need to behave, sweetheart. Because if you try anything, I'll kill him and come for you. Nod if you understand."

Penny nodded, her gaze latching onto the other man while she prayed Jake wouldn't kill either of them.

Jake kissed her on her temple, the heat of his lips burning her damp skin with a desperate heat. "I told you, I'm not leaving without my son."

He backed up, using her as a shield, and then pushed her a foot away, behind a towering pine. "Don't move, Penny. I mean it."

Confused and frightened, she scraped her knuckles against the rough bark while Jake stalked around the tree, giving her a possible means of escape. She could run now. Just leave them to duke this out. She could get Kevin and go as far away from here as possible. She'd done it before.

But the man who'd come to her rescue caused her to stay. She couldn't leave him here with Jake. He'd called her by her real name so he obviously recognized her, which could only mean they'd been digging into her past, too. Then Jake had called the man Zeke and *bro*. What did that mean? He'd never wanted to talk about himself or his family because of the classified nature of his job. None of this made any sense.

But if this man was a friend or a true brother, he hadn't come here for a family reunion. He was dressed in a bulletproof vest and wore a black cap over his crisp, dark hair that clearly read FBI. His partner was a sleek, fierce warrior. She'd always had a heart for dogs. This one was also marked as FBI.

"Hey, Penny. If you run, I'll kill him and his loyal partner, okay?" Jake said again, glancing at her with a threatening look. "But since we're all here together, I guess it would be rude of me not to make the proper introductions." He held his gun toward where the man called Zeke stood with feet braced apart and his deadly-looking rifle raised.

Before Jake could tell her who he was, the agent said, "Jake, man, don't do this. We all want to hear your side of the story. Your unit is worried about you."

This man was from Jake's unit!

"Who is he?" she asked Jake.

Keeping his eyes on the other man, Jake said, "Well, you always badgered me about my family, and now you get to meet my little brother, Zeke. Not the best of circumstances, but that can't be helped."

"You have a brother?" Penny asked, watching the man at the other end of this standoff. Hoping he could figure something out that would save both of them. He certainly looked capable. Muscular and confident, he stood ready for Jake's next move. But he also held a hint of hope that Jake would give up.

That should reassure her but…she was afraid none of them would get out of this alive.

Jake shook his head, his eyes wild, his gaze darting between her and Zeke. But he kept his pistol trained on the man and the canine. "Actually, he's only my half brother. We shared the same father but that's about it. My old man left *my* mother and *me* for his new family."

He said that with such disgust, Zeke flinched but recovered before Jake even noticed. But Penny noticed. Her heart went out to the man standing there, his rifle aimed at Jake. What must he be going through right now?

Two brothers, one good and one bad.

She couldn't walk away from this. Jake would keep coming. She had to do something now. But which one did she trust?

Jake's next words confirmed that decision and told her what she had to do. "Now you know Kevin has an uncle, but he'll never get to meet Uncle Zeke." Raising the handgun at the same time he grabbed Penny and pinned her in front of him, he said with regret in each word, "I'm going to have to kill you, bro. You know too much." His grip tightened on Penny. "You *both* know too much."

Zeke inched forward, the canine following. "Jake, think about this. Don't make things worse for yourself. Let her go and you and I can talk."

"No more talking," Jake said. Then he held the gun closer and moved it up to Penny's heart. "Back off or I'll kill her right now. I'm not playing. I have to get out of here. With Kevin."

Penny's gaze slammed into Zeke's shocked expression. She'd dropped her backpack when Jake had shoved her at the tree, and she couldn't reach it now. Panic-stricken, she looked around for a weapon. Anything would suffice. Glancing back at Zeke, she tried to send him a silent message. She made a big deal about looking past him as if she saw someone else. Straining forward, she shouted, "Jake, did you see that? I think someone's in the woods."

It was enough to cause her ex to lift his head and glance around. He shifted, his hard-edged gaze sweeping the area.

Penny slumped against him again, causing

him to shift. She slipped down and grabbed a jagged piece of rock and managed to twist toward Jake, her arm raised as she lifted the stone toward him while his arms went up in the air. She'd been a softball pitcher in high school so she could pretty much aim for any sweet spot far away. But up close, it was too hard. Thinking quickly, she aimed for the weapon in his outstretched hand. The heavy rock made contact enough against the gun for Jake to lose his grip. His gun flipped out into the air and fell a few feet away.

"You shouldn't have done that, Penny," he snapped as he shoved her onto her back and slid toward the weapon.

Zeke shouted at her, "Run. Go. Get out of here!"

The canine started barking and snarling.

Then the FBI agent shouted again, "Run!"

Penny grabbed her backpack as she headed into the woods. Her cell phone was inside. She could call the inn and warn Claire.

Gunshots went off. The FBI agent commanded, "Attack!"

Glancing back, she saw Jake roll and then hop up, the gun now aimed at the dog as he ran ahead of the barking canine, shooting to keep him away. But the dog was quick. He nipped at Jake's booted foot, his teeth sinking deep.

Her ex grunted and let out a string of curses, all the while fighting to get free of Cheetah. But his efforts failed. His pants ripped and he managed to get up and stumble forward, the dog still on his heels.

Penny couldn't stop to watch.

The whiz of a bullet hit a tree near her. She heard the shots and realized Jake was making good on his word to try to kill her.

She heard more shots and pivoted around. Her crazy ex was now shooting toward the dog.

Zeke began returning fire. The medium-sized dog was becoming more and more aggressive, barking angrily and dancing away from the continuous shots. The animal would gain on Jake again any second now. Penny turned and ducked behind a tree just as the dog leaped into the air and headed toward her assailant.

But Jake took one more shot and disappeared into the woods.

Zeke came hurrying by. "Stay there," he told her on a rushed breath.

Then Jake shouted from somewhere above her on some rocks, "Call off your partner, Zeke. I have Penny in my sights and I will take out her and the dog. You know I'm a good shot."

The words echoed out over the woods like an eerie wail. As if to prove he could do it, Jake shot above Penny's head. She ducked and held her breath.

Then she saw Jake running through the rough terrain in a zigzag pattern. Heard him shout, "I'm taking him, Penny. None of you can stop me."

He fired another round of shots, causing Zeke to rush toward Penny and push her down, his big body shielding hers.

"Halt," Zeke called to the canine barking loudly at the rock formation.

Cheetah whirled and stopped.

"Come," Zeke called again, the reluctance and frustration obvious in his tone.

The obedient dog returned and stood watch, his beautiful heavy fur quivering with awareness.

"Why did you let him go?" Penny shrieked at Zeke while she struggled to get up. But he was still blocking her, protecting her. Then she stared into his chocolate-brown eyes. The anguish she saw there only mirrored what she'd been feeling for the last few months.

Something swift and sizzling arced between them in a flash of emotion.

"I had to for now," Zeke replied softly as he placed his hands on either side of her shoulders and got up. Helping her to her feet, he added, "I know my brother. He'd shoot you and Cheetah, or he'd ambush us later. He wants you dead so he can take my nephew."

"*Your* nephew?"

"Yes," he replied, defiance in his eyes. "Kevin is my nephew. I have to get to him before Jake does."

She agreed with him there but wasn't so ready to accept him as Kevin's uncle. That sounded way too personal right now.

They'd discuss the rest of this later. "You're going after him even though you just let him slip through your fingers?" she asked, still in shock and worried about her son, still reeling from Zeke's touch and the way his dark eyes had probed her.

He placed a gentle hand on her elbow and steered her through the woods and underneath the shelter of a giant rock near a pine tree. "Right now, I'm going after Jake." Then he turned to the canine. "Cheetah, guard."

Penny looked from the dog now standing in front of her back at Zeke. "Oh, no. I'm not sitting here while my son is in danger." She tried to move past him.

Zeke held her back down. "Listen, I'm going up ahead to look for my brother, but we've got backup in the area. You need to stay here and wait for one of them to arrive, understand? Now, tell me where your son is right now so I can send someone to check on him."

Penny didn't hesitate on that. Holding her hand to her sweat-dampened hair, she said, "The Wild Iris Inn on Elk Rock Road. Just inside the town limits. Claire is the owner and she babysits for me. He's with her. I need to—"

"Stay here," Zeke commanded. "Cheetah won't let anyone come near you."

"And if your partner here gets shot?"

He pulled a handgun out of his shoulder holster. "Do you know how to use a weapon?"

She nodded. "My grandfather taught me."

"Good. Then you know what to do with this one. You've got seventeen rounds. One already in the chamber, safety off. When the magazine is empty, run as fast as you can to the main road."

With that, he took off. "Hurry," she called, thinking she'd go where she wanted after he left. "Jake could be at the inn right now. He said he had a van stashed somewhere."

"Got it," Zeke responded, already running away.

Penny tried to move but the dog moved with her. Blocking her. Feeling helpless, she searched for one of the trails. The canine gave her a daring eye-to-eye stare. Too good at his job.

Frustration gnawed at her. What more could she do? Feeling lost and so very alone, she prayed, tears falling fast and hard down her face. *Please, Lord, help me now.*

"Please don't let it be too late for my son," she said out loud. The courageous animal standing in front of her looked at her with doleful eyes, as if he understood her prayers.

Penny reached out a hand, wanting to pull her protector close. But Cheetah was trained to do what Zeke told him. He stood straight and on the alert, his eyes never leaving her face.

Then she heard what sounded like a vehicle to the east. The sound echoed over the quiet woods. Crouching, she whispered to Cheetah, "What if Jake's coming back?"

The dog turned his head toward the sound but still didn't move. Penny held her breath and listened, her adrenaline spiking. Could she really do it? Could she use this weapon to kill the father of her child?

THREE

Penny stayed crouched behind the rock, her heartbeat pounding against her temples like a jackhammer. A black van pulled up on one of the trails, and a man wielding a gun got out and scanned the woods. Penny tried to make out his face, but he was too far away and the shifting light was too low. Barely breathing, she watched as Cheetah stayed with her and stood so still she thought the dog had turned to stone. The canine emitted a low growl, the dare in that whisper of aggression telling her she was safe with him.

But the man kept coming, slowly, deliberately, as if he knew exactly where she was hiding. Penny decided she wasn't going to wait around and find out. Lifting the weighty handgun, she checked the safety and put her sights on the man. She hadn't fired a gun since Jake had taken her to target practice so long ago. Could she shoot another human being?

Taking another long look at him, she tried to memorize details of his description. He wore dark glasses and had longish, stringy blond hair. He wasn't very tall but he was brawny and in good shape.

The henchman advanced but Cheetah's growls grew louder, causing the assailant to glance up in shock and pivot back and forth. He started backing away, a definite fear in his eyes.

Penny used that fear to give her courage. Lifting up, she aimed and shot into the air near where the man stood, hoping Zeke would hear and come back. The man took off running. Cheetah's barks now turned brutal and loud.

The man hopped back in the van and started it up. Penny raised the gun again and shot toward the moving target. She missed but she thought she heard something else over the sound of the dog's barks.

The cries of a child.

Zeke followed the trail of broken bramble and loose rocks along the craggy ridge, stopping to take a photo each time he saw drops of blood on the rocks or dirt. Cheetah had at least injured his brother. Probably not a deep bite since Jake had been wearing heavy leather boots, but enough that a crime scene tech could get a sample to back up whatever Penny could tell them. The K-9 team could gather evidence and get it to Billings. They all wanted Jake.

Deciding he couldn't keep going along blindly, Zeke stopped at the top of the ridge and glanced down through the woods. It was hard to see with the growing dusk but he stilled and waited. Nothing. Jake had to be hiding down there somewhere but until help arrived, he had no choice but to turn around. He didn't want to leave Penny alone. Pivoting, he heard a crashing noise down below. Could be an animal or it could be his brother on the move again. He hurried to check it out.

The sound of gunshots in the area where he'd left Penny had him running back in that direction instead. When he heard Cheetah's fierce bark, he knew she was in trouble. Had Jake set up yet another distraction so he could get to Penny?

After what seemed like hours but had only been a few minutes, Zeke returned, winded, fatigue coloring his eyes.

Rushing up to where she sat against the tree with the gun held tightly against her, tears streaming down her face, he sank onto the ground by her. "Cheetah, sit." Then he gently cupped Penny's arms in his hands. "Are you okay?"

She handed Zeke his gun, thankful that he'd come back so quickly. But she was so scared of what she might have done it took her a while to speak. "A black van, big with no windows. A man got out and searched the area. I decided to scare him away so I shot toward him." With each word, she began to sob in earnest.

Zeke nodded, concern deepening his frown. "Good, that's good. Did you get a look at him?"

She swallowed, trying desperately to tamp down the fear that assailed her. "Yes. Not too tall. Long, stringy blond hair and glasses. And a really big rifle." Then she grabbed his shirt. "Zeke, I can't be sure since it all happened so fast and Cheetah was barking, but I… I think I heard a cry. Inside the van." The terror took over and she started shaking. "I think I heard a child crying." Then she fell against him, the sick fear engulfing her, the reality of her fears paralyzing her. "Zeke, I shot at the man and I missed. But I heard a child's cry." Pulling away, she stared up at him. "What if my son's in that van?"

Zeke's eyes went wide. Lifting her up, he pulled her closer and looked down at her. "We're going to the inn. We'll find Kevin." Then, still holding her near, he took out his phone and reported everything she'd just told him. "Yes, sir. We'll be there as soon as we can get back to my vehicle."

He ended the call and turned to her. "Let's get you back to the inn."

She tugged at his arm and pointed toward the road. "We need to go after them. They went that way. I… I have to find Kevin."

She started to go around him and tried to reach for her backpack.

"I'll get it." He snatched up the flower-encased bundle, their gazes locking for a brief moment. "Let's go."

Zeke pulled her with him across the rocky terrain at a furious trot. "My SAC—special agent in charge—Max West, and another agent are already headed to the Wild Iris, and the whole team is here and scattered throughout the woods. We've put out a BOLO on the van and we've got Jake's face plastered all over the news and social media outlets. Max made sure the locals put out an APB."

"So you didn't see him anywhere?"

"No," Zeke said. "But I did find blood on some of the rocks. I gave Max the locations so the crime scene techs can do a sweep of the area."

We had him. Penny wished they could have stopped Jake but everything happened so fast.

She prayed Kevin was safe, prayed she'd been imagining those wails. She had shot toward that van but thankfully, she'd missed.

Dear God, please, please. I couldn't bear it if my child were kidnapped. She wished this was just a horrible nightmare. Each step seemed like an eternity and each time she glanced back, she expected Jake to be trailing them.

Then she halted and gasped. "I remember something Jake said earlier."

"What?" Zeke queried, swiping at buzzing bugs.

"He said he had a van waiting. 'We'll have Kevin.' Then he went on talking about how we'd leave together."

Realization filled Zeke's eyes. "That does make it sound like Kevin would already be in the van."

She bobbed her head. "Yes, yes. I think I heard my baby crying." Putting her hands to her mouth, she tried to take another breath. "Zeke, what if Jake holding me here was all a distraction so that man could get to Kevin? And now…he could be hurt or—"

Zeke let out a frustrated sigh and took her into his arms. "Penny, think. Where did the shot land?"

She closed her eyes. "It hit a few feet in front of the van, thankfully."

"So if Kevin was in the van, he'd probably be in the back, maybe in a crib or a seat, or you could have heard something else." Softening his tone, he tucked a loose strand of hair behind her ear. "Don't think the worst until we can get to the inn, okay?"

She glanced up at him, wanting to believe him. "Okay. Hurry anyway. We need to find out."

Zeke started going over things, his voice calm while her heart screamed in agony. "We know someone else was with Jake. I have an eyewitness for that. And they were in a black van. Then you probably saw the same van. The locals and the FBI are searching for it right now."

"That person could have Kevin already and they could be leaving *right now*. Can you check? Talk to your person?"

Zeke took out his phone again and made the call. "Yes, sir. Tell them to hurry." Then he turned to her. "We've got people at the inn. We'll hear soon."

Penny felt sick, her knees weak. "Hurry, Zeke. Please. We're wasting time. He went west on the main road."

He urged her forward. "We can't get anywhere without my vehicle."

When they reached a clearing, Zeke scanned the entire area and watched his canine for any signs of a scent. The dog sniffed the air and the ground and looked toward where they'd been before.

"I'll get you there," he promised her, his eyes as dark as the tree bark. "I can't let you out of my sight now."

She nodded, glad he'd moved quickly. "I need to call Claire."

He guided her to the SUV and came around to the driver's side.

Before she could dig for her cell phone, Zeke pulled the official-looking sleek black phone out of his pocket. "Make the call."

Penny dialed the number to the inn and waited. "She's not answering. Something's wrong."

Zeke took the phone back and pressed on the gas pedal. "We'll be there in five minutes. In the meantime, we've got people already going over the area where I found you with Jake. They're searching for the van and they might find something we missed."

Penny nodded and listened while he spoke to someone about the location. She was still shaking and the blast of cold air coming from the vehicle's air-conditioning made her shiver even more. Interrupting his conversation, she said, "I think we should have tried to find the van. I can identify it. Should we turn around?"

Zeke noticed her discomfort and hit the button to turn down the airflow. After discussing the situation with his superior again, he dropped his cell phone into a cup holder between them. "I have to protect you and Kevin. He'll keep coming for you. I'm to get you to the inn first. It's too dangerous to go chasing after that vehicle."

Frustration roared through Penny. "I was right there! I should have killed that man and looked inside myself."

Zeke reached over and gripped her arm. "Listen to me, Penny. In situations like this, it's always best if the parents stay out of the way and let us do our jobs. My team is one of the best. You need to take a breath and trust us."

"I know," she said, wondering how she'd ever find her next breath. "I know." She couldn't voice the terror ripping her apart. *What if it's too late? What then?*

Zeke zoomed the sleek SUV around curves and along dirt roads and watched the rearview mirror. Cheetah stayed in the back in a roomy kennel. She felt safe with these two, but Penny couldn't relax until she knew Kevin was safe.

When they got to the Wild Iris and saw a local police officer standing with two FBI agents holding canines on leashes, her heart sank. "I have to find my baby," she cried, hopping out of the vehicle before Zeke could turn off the motor.

She ran toward the big, two-story house, every cell in her body on overload. "Kevin? Kevin, Mommy's here."

An officer stopped her at the wide stained glass front door. "Ma'am, you can't go in there."

"She's with me," Zeke said, showing the officer his ID. "Her two-year-old son could be in danger."

"He's gone," Rex Harmon said when Penny rushed inside, shaking his head. Rex, an avid hiker, had a room across from hers. "That man—he had a gun and he took the little boy."

"No!" Penny put a hand to her mouth and moaned, a sick feeling pooling inside her stomach. "No…"

"What did he look like?" Zeke asked, pulling out a picture of his half brother. "Is this him?"

"Nah," the older man said. "This thug was short and muscular with long, greasy blond hair and funky eyeglasses. He got into a beat-up old black van."

Zeke's eyes flared with awareness, his gaze

hitting on Penny. She grabbed onto a chair, her worst nightmares coming to the surface. The same man she'd seen in the woods. Kevin had been right there, inside that van. She could have saved him.

"Do you know that man?" she asked Zeke, each word a struggle, each beat of her pulse a condemnation.

He nodded. "Possibly. But we'll figure that out later."

"Was this man in the van?" Penny demanded, her finger jabbing at the picture of Jake.

"No," Rex said, sympathy in his eyes. "He was alone but he overpowered Miss Claire and hit her on the head. I heard her scream and I saw him with the boy. Miss Claire was hurt but she got to her shotgun. Only he had a gun, too, and he pointed it at the kid when we both ordered him to stop. Miss Claire dropped her gun and the man got in the van with your son and left." He glanced from the officers to Penny. "I tried to get a license plate but it was all rusted out." He gave Penny an apologetic look and waved a hand at all the officers swarming around. "I was about to call you when they showed up."

Penny's stomach twisted and recoiled. A cold sweat crept up and down her spine. She sank down on the stairs and pushed at her hair. "Is Miss Claire okay?"

"She's fine," Rex said. "She's in her room with a female officer. The EMTs looked her over but she won't go to the hospital."

Penny stood, dizziness overcoming her. Zeke reached out to her and guided her to a chair. "I'll find him. I promise. You stay here while I go and check on your babysitter."

He asked Rex to bring her some water. The front door swung open and another man wearing an FBI vest entered, along with another canine. She'd seen them outside and heard Zeke introduce him as Special Agent in Charge Max West. He had short, spiked blond hair and blue eyes that seemed to stare everyone down, but like Zeke, he seemed confident and born to be in charge. She also noticed a jagged scar on his left cheek.

That only reminded her of how dangerous this situation had become. Jake had sent someone to kidnap her son and now he was at their mercy. That man could have killed Claire and Rex, too.

She watched, impatient and numb, while FBI agents and K-9 dogs filled the inn, their presence a sharp contrast to the dainty furnishings and heirloom antiques placed all around the Victorian-style mansion turned boardinghouse.

Max West gathered all of them around and explained what would transpire next. Roadblocks, an Amber Alert, all train and bus stations made aware, all flights out of nearby airports monitored. And all agents out on the hunt.

Penny put her head in her hands and prayed. Helplessness weighed her down, a sense of doom and despair causing her to catch her breath. Why, oh, why, had she come back to Montana?

Law enforcement set up electronic equipment on every available spot and stomped over the braided rugs and slammed the stained glass doors, moving, while she sat there, frozen in a nightmare. She had to do something, *anything*, to find her little boy.

Agent West came over to her and asked her several rapid-fire questions about Jake. Did he say where he was headed? What did he look like? What kind of weapons was he carrying? Did he mention an accomplice?

He explained to her that they were aware she'd been on the run and why. They knew she'd been in a chalet in Colorado earlier in the summer. Had Jake come after her there?

Penny nodded and answered all the questions, anger warring with fear and regret. "I came back here because… I wanted my son

to be here, close to where I grew up. I thought
I was safe."

"Did you come here hoping Jake would find
you? Did he arrange to meet you out in the
Basin area?"

"No."

Fury roiled through her. Did they actually
think she'd wanted this? That she wanted to be
sitting here, paralyzed with fear, wondering if
her son was alive or dead?

Finally, Penny lifted her head and said, "He
planned to go live on a tropical island, and
he said he has a lot of money stashed somewhere but I don't know where. He wants my
son, not me. I didn't want him around Kevin,
and I sure don't want him taking my son away
from me. The man tried to kill me. Why are
you questioning me when you should be out
there searching for Kevin?"

Max West gave her a stern but sympathetic
stare. "We're doing everything we can to help
us find your son, Penny. We've taken prints
on everyone who works here or is staying
here, and we have officers going door-to-door
around this area to see if we can find any leads
or get any eyewitnesses. Don't go anywhere."

"I *know* who took my son," she said, her
voice rising. "Why aren't you listening to
me? I was an eyewitness. Up close. So close,

I feared for my life. Go and find my son before it's too late."

Zeke pulled Max aside and said something into his ear. The other man shot a frown at her. Did he know what she was afraid of, what was tearing through her racing mind?

Zeke came over and bent down in front of her. "It's highly unlikely that they'd hurt Kevin, Penny. You have to keep telling yourself that. Jake wants him, so he would order them not to harm him."

Closing her eyes to the shattering nerves breaking apart piece by piece throughout her core, she said, "Sure. And while I'm at it, I'll keep telling myself that Jake doesn't have him in that van headed to another getaway car or to the airport."

Zeke stared at her for a brief moment but one of the other agents called him. "I'll be right back." Then he whirled around. "And, Penny, don't go anywhere, understand? That would only make this worse."

Penny didn't believe it could get much worse but if they didn't do something soon, she would sneak out to her Jeep and do whatever she had to do to find Kevin. And she'd take Claire's shotgun with her.

FOUR

Fifteen minutes passed and Penny didn't think she could take another moment of waiting. Here she sat, wringing her hands, the sound of people talking around her drowned out by the emptiness clamoring inside her heart. "Kevin," she whispered, closing her eyes. "Kevin."

"Oh, honey, I'm so sorry."

She opened her eyes to find Claire Crayton gingerly stepping down the stairs, a bright red bump shining on her forehead. Claire had been so kind to Penny when she'd pulled up in the parking lot a month ago, on her last ounce of gasoline, Kevin crying in his car seat. Claire had booked them a room immediately and offered to babysit anytime Penny needed her.

"I tried to stop him but he hit me hard with his gun and I went down like a rock. Grabbed my gun but…he held the child and…" The older woman's eyes watered and her voice wobbled to a halt. "He took our precious boy. It's my fault, too."

"It wasn't your fault," Penny said, standing to wrap her hands around Claire's plump, comforting shoulders, her own eyes wet with tears, her own bruises and scratches burning from the salt. "It's my fault. I knew his daddy was dangerous, but I never dreamed he'd send a henchman to kidnap my son."

Then she started sobbing against Claire's plaid shirt, the scent of rose water and cinnamon cookies overtaking her. "I want him back, Claire. I want my little boy back."

A strong hand touched her on the arm.

Zeke.

His dark eyes held the same despair that raged through her, raw and jagged and burning. He placed her back in the nearby chair and kneeled in front of her again, his eyes on her. "Listen, we've got people out looking already, and we've put out an Amber Alert. But I need you to take me to the room where Kevin sleeps, okay? Cheetah can pick up his scent. It hasn't been that long, so if I hurry I can locate him."

"Did the others search his room?"

"Yes, but they were looking for clues regarding the kidnapper. They're searching for him while others are searching for Kevin. Both of them, really. I want to focus more on Kevin since Cheetah is trained in search and rescue." Touching a hand to her arm, he leaned in. "I promise I'm going to do everything in my power to bring Kevin back to you."

"I'm going with you to search," she said, standing and hurrying up the stairs, her heart beating just as fast as her hiking boots.

Zeke took off after her. "No."

"Yes." She stopped on the second-floor landing and turned at the first door on the left. "This is our room. I have the bedroom and he sleeps here in the living room in this crib."

Pointing to a large mahogany baby bed full of blankets and sheets decked out in a cowboy design, she walked over and picked up a stuffed brown horse, tears streaming down her face. Holding it close before she handed it to Zeke, anguish cutting through her, she said, "I'm going with you. Do you understand?"

Zeke let out a sigh, compassion in his dark eyes, and leaned down so Cheetah could get a good sniff of the worn horse. The canine lifted his snout, his ears perking up. "Yes, I understand. And since I need to keep you alive, I will go along with it. But Penny, you have to stay out of the way, okay?"

"Okay." She wiped away tears and lifted her head, staring at him with a dangerous resolve in her heart. After grabbing some baby supplies and shoving them into a diaper bag, she turned to him. "Let's go."

Zeke's head pounded with fatigue and tension ten times worse than foot soldiers stomping on his brain, but he followed Cheetah through the house and out to the SUV. Penny had insisted on gathering up some things for Kevin, including the little stuffed horse she'd clung to while the techs went over her room. Cheetah had hopefully picked up the kidnapper's scent, too, since the man had been in the house.

Zeke had to make this right.

The situation here was under control so he needed to be out there looking. The Wild Iris had become ground zero to set up operations to find Kevin and Jake. Locals and FBI alike scoured the grounds and had laptops out on top of their vehicles, searching with maps and following leads on tips. They'd had calls about sightings of three different vans in three different areas, but none of them had panned out. This could take all night. Max had assigned Nina Atkins, the petite blonde rookie who'd recently joined the team, to stay at the inn along with a couple of other agents and two locals. Nina and her K-9 partner, Sam, a cadaver-detection-trained Rottweiler, were to watch over Claire and the staff and residents. Whoever took Kevin wouldn't like leaving behind witnesses.

Claire and her crew went to work on bringing them food and drinks and offered whatever else they needed in the way of comfort. Rex answered the phone and explained the situation to the few other boarders who'd drifted in from work or travels and directed traffic to the restrooms and the coffeepot.

Vehicles kept coming and going. But no sightings had brought any substantial information, and they'd had no word on any solid leads even though the local citizens were being vigilant about helping. No one liked to hear of a child being kidnapped. Zeke couldn't let Penny see his own anxiety, but the dread pooling inside his stomach made that last cup of coffee he'd downed turn sour.

Jake was a master at setting up distractions and false scenarios. It had been one of his best assets as an agent. He'd certainly proved that today but not in a good way. Worried, Zeke knew his brother could charm just about anyone into doing his bidding.

He'd obviously gone to a lot of trouble to set things up so that while he was holding Penny and shoving her through the woods, his accomplice, Gunther Caprice, had kidnapped Kevin.

Zeke wished with all his heart he could have hauled his brother in. But even then, Gunther could have been long gone with Kevin. That thought chilled Zeke to his bones.

To make matters worse, Max wasn't too happy with him right now. Zeke had Jake in his sights and had let him get away. The whole unit probably thought he'd allowed his half brother to escape. He'd get things straight with Max and the others later. Right now, he was worried about the woman trailing behind him. Trying to get a handle of things, he studied her closely. If he was going to protect her and Kevin, he needed to figure out who exactly he was dealing with.

She was pretty in an outdoorsy kind of way. All golden skinned and toned, not an ounce of wasted fat on her. Probably worked out on a daily basis. Her hair was cut in choppy shoulder-length layers that sprouted out like waves of wheat around her triangular face. Her eyes were almond shaped and a crystal clear blue. Not piercing like Max's, but more of a clear-sky blue that reflected her heart.

And that heart was breaking right now. To be so close to her little boy and realize she'd been so near the vehicle that might have been holding him, not to mention that Kevin was somewhere with a lowlife like Gunther Caprice. No wonder the woman was in shock.

She rushed ahead of him down the stairs with her ever-present backpack and a big diaper bag over one shoulder, a staunch determination in those Montana-blue eyes.

Zeke also let Cheetah smell the baby blanket Penny had given him. Cheetah sniffed the soft wool and lifted his head to sniff the air. Then he headed to the end of the drive and sniffed around before lifting his snout toward the west.

They made it through the maze of officers and staff roaming through the quaint old house and hit the porch steps as if they were in a race against each other.

Opening the SUV's back door with a remote key, Zeke commanded Cheetah to jump in and turned to find Max West coming his way.

"Going somewhere, Agent Morrow?"

Zeke wasn't in the mood for orders. He agreed with Penny that the sooner they got out there searching, the better. "Yes, I'm going to find my nephew."

"Not so sure that's a good idea," Max said. "You do know we have people out there already searching, right?"

Zeke didn't want to be argumentative but he would stand his ground. "Cheetah has the boy's scent, sir, and you know he's trained for this. I need to find Kevin while the trail is fresh." Then he leaned in. "As I told you in my report, I think we're looking for Gunther Caprice. He fits the description that science teacher gave me earlier and the description Rex gave us. The man saw him drive away from the basin in a black van. And later, Penny saw the same man, same vehicle, just like I told you."

Caprice used to be third in line with the Dupree clan and had once been chummy with Violetta Dupree—sister to the crime brothers—but he'd fallen on hard times and broke off with them when the FBI had captured Reginald Dupree in a raid close to six months ago. His uncle Angus had gotten away, taking Jake with him, but now Angus was dead. That left a lot of people scattered and scared. Had Gunther joined up with Jake for money or for revenge? Jake had edged him out, after all.

If Jake's accomplice was in fact Gunther Caprice, they could get a wealth of information out of that man. He'd been missing and wanted for questioning for months and now, suddenly, he was back in the picture. Jake had obviously made him an offer he couldn't refuse. But Gunther couldn't be trusted to keep Kevin alive. That lowlife was only out to save his own sorry hide.

Max's phone buzzed and he held up a hand and took the call, indicating he wasn't through with this conversation. "Is that right?" He eyed Zeke. "I've got an agent about to leave now." He ended the call and turned to Zeke. "Your timing is perfect. A man and woman on a motorcycle heard the reports and spotted a black van about five miles from here, driving west on Old Fork Road out of town."

Penny gasped when she heard their conversation from her spot by the passenger door, her gaze slamming into Zeke's. "That has to be him."

"I'm on it," Zeke said. "Cheetah sniffed the spot where the van was parked here and he's already tracking in that direction."

"You'll take backup." Max motioned to another agent, who hurried over. After explaining the situation to team member Harper Prentiss, who held her German shepherd, Star, on a leash, Max nodded and pinned Penny with a solemn stare. "Miss Potter, you really should stay here and wait—"

"I'm going to find my son," she said, the resolve in her words and eyes telling Max they couldn't stop her. "I can't sit here and wait, and you can't make me."

Zeke glanced at Max. "I'd feel better if I can keep an eye on her, sir."

"Morrow, we have eyes on her now and it's safer if she stays here—"

"Stop arguing about me," Penny interjected. "We're running out of time. I'm going to find Kevin, with or without either of you."

Max West looked from Zeke to Penny, surprise and a grudging acceptance in his expression. "Well, I *won't* feel better but… I'm holding you responsible for her, Zeke." He lifted a hand. "Go. Do what you have to do and this time if you find Jake, don't let him get away."

Zeke nodded and opened the door for Penny, now fully aware that his superior did think he had *purposely* let his half brother slip through his fingers. And maybe he had. He could have let Cheetah corner Jake or continue to go after him. But his K-9 partner needed to stay with Penny while Jake tried to ascertain which direction Jake might have gone. When he'd found only footprints and bloodstains on those rocks, he knew Jake had been nearby.

Had he made the right call, giving up the chase to run back to Penny? He'd heard enough about Jake lately to understand his brother would kill anyone or anything to get what he wanted. He remembered that dark side of Jake, had seen it come out at the oddest times. Jake would have shot Penny without any remorse.

A while back, he'd tied up Harper in a cave in Colorado, and after telling her he was corrupt and he liked having money and power, he'd left her there where she could have died if she hadn't ordered K-9 Star to chew apart the ropes holding her. Jake had no qualms about killing a canine or a human.

Zeke had to protect the woman Jake had threatened to kill. He'd made the only choice he could, but now he had a second chance to capture his traitorous brother and see justice done.

Penny got in the SUV, a look of relief mixed with the anxiety marring her expression. "Thank you."

"For what?" he asked gruffly.

"For standing up to your boss."

"I wasn't just standing up to him," Jake replied. "I meant it when I said I plan to protect you. No matter what."

She shot him a surprised but grateful look. "I appreciate that but right now you need to find my little boy."

"I'm going to."

Zeke checked with Max again, hoping for any reports that could help. "I've got Cheetah by an open window and we're heading west, sir. Old Fork Road. We're on the road now but nothing yet."

"Stay on it and be careful," Max replied. "I'll send backup if you and Harper need it." Then he added, "Zeke, I know he's your brother and you want to keep him alive but—"

"I understand," Zeke bit out. "I know my duty, Max."

He ended the call and slung his phone into a cup holder.

"I'm surprised they haven't yanked you off this case," Penny said. "It must be hard, tracking him down like this."

"My job," Zeke retorted, wondering if she wanted to pick a fight.

She didn't say anything else and he regretted being sharp with her. "It's not easy but… if I can get to him first I might be able to take him in instead of—"

"Killing him," she finished. Then she went silent again.

Zeke had to wonder how she felt about that. Did she still love Jake in spite of everything?

Anxious to get this over with, Zeke turned the truck toward the west and started searching for the road they needed. He prayed they'd also find the thug who'd taken Kevin before the man could meet up with Jake Morrow. Because if that happened, he feared they might not ever see Penny's son again.

FIVE

Zeke tried to keep her talking while he kept watch on Cheetah in the back, his snout searching the air and the woods rolling by. He told Penny he needed to hear her story and gather any details she might remember. But she knew he was just as curious about her as she was about him. He obviously didn't trust her since she'd been involved with Jake. She couldn't blame him for that. Look where it had gotten her.

"How did you meet Jake?"

She swallowed and held tight to the bottle of water in her hand, memories she'd tried to bury coming to the surface. "I'm a wilderness guide," she said, her voice raw and low. How could she talk about this when Kevin was out there, afraid and in the clutches of dangerous criminals? But she did talk. Anything to keep from crawling out of her skin. "We literally ran into each other a couple of years ago on a hiking trail."

"He hiked a lot," Zeke recalled. "All over the world."

Shooting Zeke a quick glance, she added, "He wasn't out on a leisurely hike that day. He told me he was a federal agent and explained how it could get dangerous for me to be in the area." She smiled but it hurt to do so since every muscle in her body was coiled like rappelling rope. "But he hurried back and asked for my phone number, in case I saw anyone suspicious. He called me the next night but it wasn't regarding the case."

Looking straight ahead, she said, "We were inseparable after that. He had some downtime once he finished the case and...we spent two weeks together, hiking, kayaking and fishing. He even made me practice my shooting skills. But after I had Kevin, I didn't want a gun in the house."

She stopped, gulping in the air she couldn't seem to find. "I don't want to go down memory lane, Zeke. It hurts too much. Can't you make this SUV go any faster?"

Zeke reached out and squeezed her hand. "Penny, don't think about that shot you made. You didn't know—"

"I should have been more careful," she

choked out. "I can't get the sound of those cries out of my mind."

"The noise could have scared Kevin," he said. To reassure her, he added softly, "Besides, we haven't confirmed that Kevin is with the suspect."

She shook her head and wiped her eyes. "I should know. A mother would feel that and when I heard that baby cry out, I knew in my heart it was Kevin. Jake would at least get Kevin to a doctor if he's hurt, right?"

"I have to believe that, yes," Zeke said, the look in his eyes full of concern. "Jake wasn't always this bad. Obviously, you saw some of the good in him."

She shot Zeke an anguished look. "He sweet-talked me into seeing the good, yes. Which makes me pathetic."

"He always was a sweet-talker," Zeke said. "Jake has charisma and he can persuade people with a flash of his dimples. He usually had a pretty girl hanging on his arm."

Penny took in a breath at hearing that. "I certainly fell right into that pattern with him. I ignored that nagging feeling in my heart that made me question his long absences and all the secrecy. He was probably off having flings with other women the whole time he was with me."

Zeke shot her an apologetic stare. "I'm sorry,

I shouldn't have said that. I don't know much about his escapades except what he deemed fit to tell me."

"It's okay," she replied, her head down. "I've turned my life around because of Kevin. My faith is strong now. I can overcome what Jake did to me but right now, I want to find my son."

Stopping between two roads, Zeke glanced back to where Cheetah sniffed the air again. When he seemed satisfied that they were still on the right path, Zeke turned southwest and said, "Jake fooled me, too. For a while there after he joined the FBI, he had me thinking we could be true brothers. Even encouraged me to follow in his footsteps to become a law officer."

"He never mentioned you," Penny said, wishing she'd known all of this from the beginning. She could have reached out to Zeke and maybe helped with the search for Jake. But instead, she'd run away like a coward.

You were trying to protect Kevin.

But she'd failed at that when she'd returned here.

If she'd reported Jake's demands to the authorities all those months ago, she might not be searching for her son right now.

That realization made her blurt out one of the things gnawing at her. "I have to wonder if Jake contacted me that last time only to get information on whether your team was searching for him. He asked a few pointed questions about anyone coming around to see me, but he promised he'd take care of us. I'm not used to depending on a man but I sure wanted to believe him. For a while I did believe him." Pushing her fingers through her hair, she said, "But everything changed."

"How so?" Zeke asked, his eyes on the road.

She took a sip of water. "He called one day out of the blue but sounded kind of off, you know? He kept referring to his days at Quantico and how this job meant so much to him, how people trusted him and depended on him. Then he said something else that struck me as odd. He said he'd lost trust in the FBI and his connections at Quantico and he wasn't sure about anything anymore. He wasn't sure of his next step. And that's not like Jake."

"No, it's not. But I can see him wanting to be able to take care of you, so maybe not being able to do that had him worried," Zeke said, his gaze sliding over her face. "You're pretty and capable. Jake likes strength in women. He must have admired that about you."

"I don't feel so strong," she whispered, another distant memory nagging at her. She'd doubted Jake's faithfulness to her many times and thinking of Quantico only reminded her of that. She was pretty sure he'd been close to someone he'd gone through training with since she'd found a picture in some of his stuff. One of him with a female recruit. But when she'd asked him about it, he refused to talk to her about anything related to work. She sighed, knowing she should mention this to Zeke, but she wasn't ready to share yet another shameful truth with him.

Pushing all that away, she said, "As I said before, I'm tired of going down memory lane. I want my son back." The ache of not knowing if Kevin was okay cut like a knife slowly slashing at her insides.

"We'll find the man who took Kevin," Zeke promised. "Cheetah can pick up vapor scents in the air and any other kind of scent on the ground. He's a smart, highly trained K-9 officer. One of the best."

Penny looked back at Cheetah. The furry dog gave her a long stare to reassure her. She knew Zeke was trying hard to keep her sane, but right now her insides burned with a raw ache and every nerve in her body hummed with the need to find her child.

"Why don't you tell me what you think about Jake?" she asked, hoping to take her mind off the horror of not having her son with her. "Did he and his mother get along?"

"He used to say Velma Morrow was weak," Zeke said. "She died a few years ago and Jake barely made it to the funeral. He left right after the service and after that, things seemed to shift between us. We stayed close but his moods changed like quicksilver, so I never knew what to expect with him."

Penny could relate to that. "He was moody and he'd hold everything inside. I never knew what he'd been through. He talked about a few friends he'd made along the way, but nothing too revealing." She blew out a frustrated breath. "I wish he'd told me about his past. About you. You'd think he'd mention having a half brother and that you worked for the FBI, too."

"He's always been secretive," Zeke said. "But now he's in a bad way. Too late for him to turn this around."

He sounded almost sympathetic, but Penny refused to feel sorry for Jake right now.

"According to my mom, our dad was also moody and easy to anger," Zeke continued. "But he could be a real charmer when he wanted something. He was a successful lawyer and my mom worked in his law firm as a secretary. She fell hard for him but she didn't know he was married. It was a real mess. He left Jake's mother and after they divorced, he married mine but left when I was too young to understand. I found out I had a brother one night when they were arguing about it."

"And…is your mother still alive?"

"Yes. She lives in Salt Lake City. I don't see her much."

Penny didn't press him on that. Her heartbeat echoed with each bump in the rugged lane. They'd only been on the road for about fifteen minutes, but it seemed like hours to her. What if they didn't get to Kevin in time? "I… I need to find Kevin, Zeke. My son shouldn't have to pay for Jake's criminal activities."

"And neither should you." Zeke's expression became etched with slashes of remorse. "You fell in love with him when he still had some good in him. Kevin is part of that good."

Penny teared up again. "Kevin is so precious. He's my entire world. I changed my life and found my faith again because I wanted to be the best mother possible. I miss him. I don't know what I'll do if anything has happened to him."

"Even if Jake has him, he won't hurt Kevin," Zeke said, trying to reassure her. "You have to keep telling yourself that."

Penny stared ahead. "He wasn't happy about

my pregnancy at first but once Kevin was born, he changed and tried to be a good father to him. I have to remember that. And... at first he seemed to love me, too."

Zeke shook his head. "That sounds like Jake. He always loved the ladies but I'm thinking he saw something special in you. You gave him a son."

"But he didn't love *me* enough to stay," she lamented, tears she refused to shed burning at her eyes. "He would come and go and he made me promise to never mention him to anyone because of his work. But now I think he didn't want anyone to know about us, either. I thought we had something solid between us but when I refused to leave with him, he turned ugly. Almost desperate."

"He *is* desperate." Zeke slowed the truck and let Cheetah do his thing. "That's why we have to be careful."

Looking out over the meadows and woods around the basin, she said, "He promised me a lot of things but none of those promises came to pass. He would come and visit Kevin, though, just pop in and out, usually late at night and gone by morning. He'd send toys and mail cash in envelopes with no return address. With just one note. 'For my son.'"

She lowered her head and raked her hands

through her tumble of hair. "The money helped but his callous nature was a slap in the face. It showed me exactly what he thought of me."

Now she felt even more ashamed and disappointed, knowing the cash was dirty mafia money; knowing that the father of her child would stoop to kidnapping Kevin and possibly taking him away from her forever.

Zeke looked as if he wanted to comfort her but she knew he had to stay on task. "When did you talk to him last? Has he been in contact with you over the last few months?" he asked.

"Only once, no, twice," she said, turning to face him. "A few months ago, he texted and said he wouldn't be by for a while since he was involved in a heavy case that required top secrecy and a lot of travel."

"The Dupree crime family," Zeke stated. "He went deep undercover and somehow, he never came out."

"I didn't hear from him for a while but about five months ago, I got a package in the mail. It was a little stuffed horse. The card attached said 'For my son.'"

Zeke's eyes widened. "The one you packed and brought with us? Jake sent it?"

She nodded. "He called me a month after that and told me to pack a bag and get Kevin ready. We were leaving the country." Shaking her head, she looked back at Cheetah, wishing the dog would signal something, anything. "I refused and hung up. I knew he was in trouble and I didn't want to risk getting involved or taking Kevin out of the country. So I left the Elk Basin and moved around from state to state, finding odd jobs where I could. After I saw a news report about all this, I thought he'd be long gone by now. I wanted to bring Kevin home but someone else was in the house I rented, so we found a new home at the Wild Iris. I'd only planned to stay there a few days but...we love it there." She stopped and put a hand to her lips. "We *did* love it there."

Zeke pinned her with a hard glare. "Why did you return *here* knowing Jake was still on the run? Were you hoping he'd come for you? Maybe take you with him after all?"

She glared back at him, heat washing over her. "Is that what you think? You all keep asking me that. Did I look like I wanted to go with him this afternoon when he had that gun on me? Do I seem happy about the fact that he might have my son on a plane right now?"

"I'm sorry." He shrugged and revved the truck. "I have to know the truth."

"The only truth you need right now is that I love my son and I'd never do anything to put him in jeopardy. That's why I left, to protect Kevin. As for Jake, I was hoping he was somewhere on the other side of the world." Leaning her head against the window, she sighed. "Now I wish *I'd* left the country. My son might be with me right now if I had."

SIX

Before Zeke could reassure her that it wasn't her fault, they arrived at Old Fork Road and Cheetah held his furry head out the back-side window and lifted his snout. Zeke skidded and turned onto the dirt lane and brought the SUV to an abrupt halt.

"Stay here," he told Penny while he checked his 9 mm handgun and grabbed his high-powered rifle. Harper pulled her SUV up behind him and came around with Star.

"Max is sending the locals, too," she said, probably to warn Zeke to be alert.

Zeke didn't argue with her. He wanted this over. "Cheetah's on fire, so let's go."

"Jake will get away if he hears sirens," Penny cautioned as she rounded the vehicle. "What are you doing?"

"I told you—"

But she wasn't listening. She headed into the woods, her hiking boots hitting against vines and bramble. She'd been antsy on the ride over here and now she was evidently in full warrior-mama mode.

Zeke did an eye roll toward Harper and took off, trailing Penny while he tried to follow Cheetah. Harper and Star had his back and they had a whole police department on the way.

He let Cheetah take the lead and followed him without hesitation. Search and rescue was Cheetah's specialty but the loyal dog had been at it all day. Zeke knew his K-9 partner wouldn't quit until he did, so he kept going. They finally caught up with Penny. She seemed to be wandering aimlessly, a desperate fear in her demeanor.

Whirling when she heard them approaching, she gazed over at Zeke, a tremor in her words. "What's wrong with me? I know these woods. I do. I should be able to see the signs of someone walking through here. A broken branch, a footprint in the dirt. But… I don't know where to start, where to go."

Zeke stilled Cheetah then reached out to lay a comforting hand on Penny's arm. "You have to trust me. I'll show you."

Her gaze moved over him as if she were searching for shards of his brother. "Okay." She calmed down and focused on getting her bearings, but Zeke heard the trembling in her voice. Scanning the surrounding area, she said, "I don't know this area as well as the one along the basin. This is more overgrown and less used. Not many trails but lots of places to hide out."

Then she took off toward some bramble. "Look." Pointing to where the heavy bushes and brush had been knocked down, she whirled. "I think they must have gone through here."

Zeke clasped her hand to keep her from crashing through the forest again. "I know you're scared and worried. I'm concerned, too. But the first twenty-four hours are the most crucial, and we've got the best people we could ask for out searching everywhere."

Penny nodded, her eyes misty. "I get that and I'm thankful for it, but I'm telling you, I think they went this way. This shows fresh tracks. It could have been from an animal but... I think we need to detour down into this incline."

Taking out a flashlight, Zeke studied the broken bramble and footprints in the dust and commanded Cheetah to sniff the dirt. The dog moved his snout over the path before turning back to Zeke.

"It seems you were right," he said, proud

of Penny for keeping her head in spite of the agony he saw in her eyes. He wanted to hug her close, but that would go beyond duty and the urgency they both felt.

She turned back toward the path, her fingers dashing tears away. "Hurry."

Together they worked their way through the dense forest. Cheetah lifted his snout in the air, following the vapor scent and the foot trails that had brought them here. With the sun sliding closer to the horizon toward the west, the woods were becoming dusky and shadowed.

They made their way into an overgrown hollow where a rutted, jagged path led down a short incline. A perfect hiding spot. But why would the kidnapper bring Kevin into the woods?

Maybe the man had been trying to escape but had parked the van and come here to hide out and avoid the roadblocks?

When he heard stomping feet about twenty yards away, Zeke stopped and silently called Cheetah back. A man started shouting, obviously talking to someone on his phone. Penny lifted up, already scanning the woods ahead. Zeke grabbed Penny and held her against him, a finger to his lips. Then he leaned close and pointed toward the area below. "If you want your son back, let me do my job."

She nodded, tears forming in her eyes. But she stayed still and silent and followed a few steps behind him.

Zeke gave Cheetah a hand signal to keep quiet while they listened. The man went into a rant. "I got the kid but the heat's on, man. You need to get out here and get your brat. I left two live witnesses at that inn and I got shot at in the woods with some snarling animal nearby. I need to leave right now. It ain't safe. You'd better get in touch with your contact in Colorado. I hate Montana and I hate dogs."

He gave jittery directions to the location and turned toward the cluster of bushes where Zeke and Penny were hiding.

Penny's slight gasp caused Zeke to look over at her. She put a hand to her mouth and took a deep breath. The kidnapper didn't seem to hear. He whirled and started pacing again.

Zeke turned back to study the kidnapper's face and immediately recognized the man. Gunther Caprice. Motioning for Penny to get down, he rushed toward the man, Cheetah deadly silent beside him. Spotting Kevin sitting forlorn and confused in some leaves, Zeke breathed a sigh of relief but he didn't stop.

"FBI. Turn around now!" Then he gave Cheetah the attack command.

The surprised man pulled out a gun and

whirled into the bushes, quickly firing off a round of shots. He barely missed Cheetah as the dog leaped toward the dense cluster of scrub oaks and rocks near where he had Kevin hidden.

"Halt," Zeke called, hoping to keep the suspect alive for questioning. But he was also concerned that Kevin could get caught up in a shoot-out.

The man fired again, the bullet hitting inside some bushes near Zeke.

Zeke brought Cheetah back and took cover but Penny took off at a run and skirted around trees and bushes before he could stop her. He kept shooting at the man to cover her and watched as she grabbed up her frightened, crying toddler and took off in a sprint into the shadowy woods.

A wave of panic and fury surged through him. What was she *thinking*? She could get lost out there or worse, run right into Jake's arms. Zeke couldn't go after her right now.

Zeke heard Harper behind him on her phone, calling in their location, and hoped Jake would be listening in on the radio and come anyway. He'd either rush out here, or he'd hear the scanner alert and sirens and go in the other direction.

But his brother wanted Kevin. That incentive might flush him out.

Zeke had to get to Penny and Kevin, but he couldn't let Gunther get away.

"Drop your weapon, Caprice!" Zeke called out again. "We have you surrounded."

The man kept shooting but took off toward where Penny had gone. Zeke could hear Kevin's fearful wails off in the distance. He called out to Harper. "Stay on him. I have to find Penny and Kevin."

Harper nodded and shouted at Star to search, but when Zeke heard a vehicle cranking up in the distance beyond the tree line, he feared not only had the suspect gotten away but he might have taken Penny and Kevin, too.

Zeke ordered Cheetah to search. They took off in the direction of where he'd last heard the wails. Zeke hoped Cheetah would find his nephew quickly so they could whisk Kevin to safety. Zeke gave the eager canine a long leash. Cheetah sniffed here and there but the loyal dog was running out of steam, so Zeke gave him water and hand-fed him food to keep him going.

Thirty minutes in with constant communication with Max and the team, and still no sign of Caprice or Penny and Kevin.

Where had Penny taken the boy? And had

the suspect taken both of them? As the sun sank behind the trees, a solid fear hammered against Zeke's heart. He radioed Harper again. "Anything?"

"Negative," she reported back. "The boss and the locals are searching the other side of the ridge where we heard a vehicle starting, but we think the kidnapper disappeared on foot or had another getaway vehicle pick him up. We spotted the old van but nothing there." She released a breath. "We've swiped it for fingerprints, but whoever this is knows how to work around that. Star alerted on a spot where we found what looked like four-wheeler or Rhino tracks. Probably how they got away but we can't be sure at this point. I'm sorry, Zeke."

"No sign of the woman and the boy here, either," Zeke reported, wondering if Jake could be listening in. He signed off and kept stalking through the heavy foliage. Soon it would be breeding season for elk in these woods, and even this early it could be dangerous. An elk could easily kill a woman or a child.

Zeke often prayed when he was out on a mission like this one. He'd grown used to the evil in the world, but this hit too close to home. At a young age, Zeke had found out he had a brother and so he'd tried to get to know

Jake, but his mother had explained things pretty bluntly.

"Jake Morrow doesn't want to be your friend or your brother. Your father used women, son. He convinced me he loved me and I believed him. But he couldn't handle leaving his first wife for me and so…he just left all of us. He always wanted more. More money. More power. More women. No one could ever please the man."

At times such as this when he had to be on high alert and at his best, Zeke often thought about his dad. Was he still alive? Did he regret leaving his two sons or the women he'd hurt so badly? Zeke fought against becoming that kind of man. He wouldn't be that way, not after what they'd all been through.

Now he wondered why Jake had turned bad. But his mother had always warned him. "Jake has a mean streak and an appetite for the finer things in life, just like your father. He can be conniving when he wants something. You'd be wise to stay away from him."

Zeke had chalked that advice up to bitterness after he and Jake had become close, but now he had to wonder if his mother had been right.

"He left my mom for yours," Jake used to

say with a dark frown. "What kind of man does that?"

Zeke could never answer that question. But he'd burned with the need to be a better man than his father. He'd joined the church at an early age and while he and Jake saw each other occasionally and he longed for his brother to join him at church functions, it had never happened. Jake had made fun of Zeke's strong faith and later had even teased Zeke about copying him and trying to outdo him by becoming first a K-9 cop and later joining the FBI. Zeke had taken it in stride since he looked up to Jake during those couple of years when they'd had a little bit of a bond. Now he could see that Jake had resented him from the beginning.

Now it had all come down to this.

Jake was on the run and Zeke was trying to save the mother of his child.

Why had she run?

Because she didn't trust any of them. And how could he blame her after what she'd been through?

Determined to find her, Zeke spurred Cheetah on and once they'd circled back and tried a different path, the dog became excited and took off to the east. Had she been moving in circles to throw them off?

Twenty minutes later, they'd made their way back to Zeke's vehicle but there was still no sign of Penny and Kevin.

Until Cheetah quietly alerted at the SUV, his ears and head up and his gaze bouncing back to Zeke in a sure sign that he'd located a possible friendly.

Or it could be Jake or the thug inside there, but Cheetah wasn't indicating danger.

Zeke praised the anxious canine, then carefully opened the driver's-side door, his gun drawn, to peek in the back where the tinted windows kept anyone from seeing inside. Penny lay curled up next to Cheetah's kennel, her son beside her while she shielded him with her body.

The sight of them hiding in such a tight space just about undid Zeke. But the dark windows and the padded kennel were a perfect camouflage. He commanded Cheetah to stay. "Penny, it's me. Zeke. You're both safe now."

She lifted her head, exhaustion shadowing her eyes in the setting sun. "Did you find Jake?"

Kevin's sleepy eyes opened and he sat up. "Doggy?"

Zeke smiled at that but shook his head in answer to Penny. "Not yet."

"Then we're not safe, no matter what you keep telling me."

She was right. Zeke had to protect his nephew. And her. "What do you want me to do?" he asked, knowing it really wasn't up to him or her right now.

She pushed at her hair and rubbed a gentle hand over her curious toddler. "My grandfather has a cabin deep in the woods on the other side of the basin. He left it to me but I never told Jake about it because I don't get over there very much. But I'm going to take Kevin there."

She was not asking for his permission.

Zeke understood but he wouldn't back down, either. "Then I'm going with you, but you have to come up front so Cheetah can get into his kennel."

She shifted and tried to lift Kevin.

"Hold on," Zeke said, rushing around to the back of the vehicle to pop open the automatic door. "Let me."

"Hey, Kevin," he said, offering the boy his outstretched arms. "I'm your Uncle Zeke."

Kevin looked confused but when he saw Cheetah, his eyes lit up. "Doggy." Glancing back at Penny, the little boy giggled.

"That's Cheetah," Zeke said.

He reached in and took Kevin into his arms, the feel of the little boy's sweaty, sweet skin hitting against all his protective gear and breaking the shell around his heart.

"Mama, Cheety," Kevin echoed, glancing back at Penny.

"I've got him," Zeke said, reaching out his free hand to Penny.

She took it, her eyes meeting his, an unspoken understanding threading between them. "You had the keys or I'd already be gone."

"Well, then I'm glad I had the keys. And I'm also glad I left it unlocked."

He was about to break every rule in the book but he wasn't going to take her back out there. Not when Jake was still on the run and after his son. So he called Max and gave him the report. "Kevin and Penny are safe and they're with me, sir. Gunther Caprice is the kidnapper. He's working with Jake. He mentioned a contact in Colorado."

"Where are you now?"

Zeke took a breath. "I'm on my way to a place where Penny already planned to go anyway, with or without me. I'm going into hiding with Penny and Kevin while I figure out what to do next. And you won't hear from me until I have a plan."

"Negative," Max said. "Morrow, you bring her in now."

Zeke ended the call, Max's warning command echoing in his head. He had to ignore the SAC, at least for tonight. Right now, he had to follow his heart instead of protocol.

He'd ask for forgiveness later. And deal with the fallout then, too.

SEVEN

"We're here," Penny said, pointing to the dark house looming up near a narrow ridge. "This is the Potter cabin."

Zeke drove at a snail's pace while he glanced over the dark woods. "Secluded and definitely off the beaten path."

"I'm not sure what we'll find," Penny admitted, apprehension bouncing off her. She took in the long front porch and the square, squatty home that had been in her family for generations. Her grandfather was her champion and he'd taught her how to survive in these woods and hills. He'd died a year before Kevin was born. Her son was named after him.

But this place that had once been a haven now looked sinister and intimidating. What if someone was lying in wait out here? They'd be ambushed and…her son could be taken again.

Earlier when she'd found Kevin, an overwhelming rush of relief had swept through her. But she knew they didn't have a second to spare. Desperate, she'd zigzagged through the woods and hurried back to Zeke's SUV, hoping to get in it and drive away. No keys, but it had been open. So she'd hidden her scared little boy in the best spot available. Now she still marveled that other than a few scratches and bug bites, Kevin seemed okay. She would not let him out of her sight again. But being in this isolated spot only reminded her of what she'd been through today.

Panic gripped her like a set of claws, choking off the air she needed to inhale. "Zeke, I don't know about this. I mean, it's overgrown and run-down. Maybe we should—"

He touched her arm, the strength in his hand warm and sure. "Hey, take another breath. Kevin is with us now. This will do until we can get to safety in the morning." He scanned the surrounding woods. "Cheetah and I will do a thorough check of both the house and the area."

Penny tamped down her trepidations. They didn't have much of a choice. "I came here for a while before I went on the run and cleaned it and thought about staying but...having a cabin in the woods isn't fun when you're alone and afraid for your child. Or when your ex-boyfriend isn't happy with you."

"It won't be fun when you're in hiding, either," Zeke replied, sympathy sounding in the words. "But it'll keep us safe. We'll make sure of that."

He parked the dark vehicle around back where a lean-to held rotting firewood and some rusty gardening tools. Penny surveyed the overgrowth around the cabin and tried not to think about rattlesnakes or salamanders. Or scorpions and spiders. She was so exhausted, every muscle in her body screamed for relief. But she was too keyed up to relax now. Kevin was asleep in her arms since they didn't have a proper car seat. And maybe because she didn't want to let go of him ever again.

"Stay here while Cheetah and I check things out," Zeke said, his tone firm. Then he handed her a flashlight. "Use this if you get concerned. Flash the light and check out the darkness. Or use it as a weapon."

Penny nodded. "The key is hidden over the right windowsill near the front door."

While Zeke and Cheetah walked through the shifting shadows, she sank back in the dark SUV with a heavy sigh. She could finally let out the breath she'd been holding and try to calm herself. She prayed, thanking God and asking Him to protect them. Surely Jake wouldn't find them here.

Zeke had been careful getting them out of danger. He'd taken back roads and crisscrossed around the many trails and old routes. She'd shown him some off-the-beaten-path roads that didn't qualify as safe in most people's minds. They'd hurried into an old general store about ten miles to the south and gathered a few supplies. No one was around, the place didn't have security cameras and the manager didn't even look up at them.

Surely her baby would be safe for a while.

She clung to Kevin, her heart pounding against his, her fears subsiding for a brief few minutes. When a dark figure came around the corner, she almost gasped. But it was Zeke.

"It's secure around the immediate perimeter. Let's get inside."

Zeke had become more and more brusque as day turned to night. He didn't want to be here taking care of her, obviously. He probably wanted to be out there on the hunt for his brother. The father of her son.

He wouldn't do a lot of talking tonight unless it was to grill her more about Jake. But she didn't know anything much more beyond what she'd already told him. Zeke was so different from his half brother. Dark and brooding and serious but so solicitous of her son.

And her. He was risking a lot, going into hiding with them.

He wanted justice. He was the good side of Jake. She hoped.

When he took Kevin out of her arms and held his big hand to her sleeping son's head to steady the child against his shoulder, hot tears pricked at Penny's tired eyes. Kevin would be safe with Zeke.

Zeke cared about Kevin. It was that simple. And he'd been forced to bring her along while he tried to protect his nephew.

She thanked God for that and said a prayer for Zeke as she followed the man shielding her son into the darkness of the old cabin, the musky scents of aged furniture and stale tobacco smoke hitting her in a full-force rush of dry air. Granddaddy Potter had been a heavy smoker. That had certainly contributed to his early death. And she'd never been able to clear the air completely, no matter how many candles and air fresheners she'd tried.

"Electricity?" Zeke asked, his flashlight out and on. He handed it to her so he could hold on to Kevin.

"Nope. But we have kerosene lanterns and candles. I usually open the windows to bring in fresh air, but I guess that's out of the question for now."

"Yes. We'll just have to hope the air cools down for the night."

"Kevin is exhausted," she said. "I don't know if he'll even wake up to eat any dinner."

"I should lay him down," Zeke said, glancing around.

"Not before I check the bedding and the sofa."

She hurried and found a lantern and some matches. On the third try, she had the lantern burning bright into the corners and used the flashlight to check more thoroughly.

While Zeke stalked behind her, Kevin safe in his arms and Cheetah watching with fascination, she gingerly lifted the old mattress and pulled out sofa cushions. A few dead bugs and scrambling spiders, but nothing too much to worry about.

She whirled around after shaking cushions and fluffing pillows. "Let's lay him on his blanket on the couch for now. I'll find the sheets for the bed and get it covered."

"I'll take the couch later then," Zeke said. "Cheetah and I can watch out the window from that location."

She nodded, glad the cabin only had one big window in the living area and a small window over the sink. Tugging Kevin's favorite blanket and his cherished "Wittle Horsey" stuffed animal out of his diaper bag, Penny breathed deep, the smell of clean soap assaulting her. Her baby's smell—sweet and pure and innocent. To think how close she'd come to losing him.

"How did I let this happen?" she asked, not even realizing she'd said it out loud.

"You didn't let anything happen," Zeke replied. "Jake took advantage of you, same way he's been using people all his life. It's finally caught up with him."

She didn't want to analyze that observation right now so she swiped and dusted with one of the baby wipes she had in the diaper bag, expending what little energy she had left. Satisfied that the old leather couch was clean and safe, she motioned for Zeke to place Kevin on the superhero blanket, a threadbare sofa pillow at his head. After kissing Kevin and hearing him sigh when she snuggled the worn little stuffed animal next to him, she turned back to Zeke, her need to nest kicking in.

"Let's get this place cleaned up. I'll make us some soup."

"Okay." He ordered Cheetah to stay and the dog circled and sat down by the sofa. With his dark eyes on Kevin, Cheetah curled up as close to Kevin as he could possibly get.

That brought her a new measure of comfort. Her son had two fierce protectors. Penny felt a new sense of hope. Maybe they just might make it out of this alive.

Zeke found a broom and started sweeping away dust bunnies and spiderwebs. "Tell me about your grandfather."

Penny grabbed the matchbox and managed to get the old two-burner propane stove working. "Don't you already know everything about me?"

"We did some research and a background check," he admitted. "But I want to hear it from you."

She opened the large can of chicken noodle soup. "Why? What does it matter now?"

He kept sweeping, the gleaming low light of the old lantern casting shadows before him like scattering leaves. "It matters to me," he said, stopping to stare into her eyes. "We're here together. Might as well get to know each other."

She stirred the soup and found crackers and two chunky mugs. After rinsing the mugs with a little bottled water, she deemed them sterile enough. Was this his way of making sure she was a fit mother to his nephew? That caused a new fear to spring into her mind. "Are you going to take Kevin away from me?"

Zeke whirled, both hands gripping the old broom, his eyes even darker in the glow from the kerosene lamp. "No. Why would you even think that?"

Penny turned down the burner and took their mugs to the old table. "I don't exactly qualify for mother of the year. I thought maybe—"

"You thought wrong," he said, a tremor of anger in his words. He finished sweeping dirt and grime into the dustpan and turned to toss it out beyond the screen door. "I wouldn't do that to you or to Kevin. I know what it's like to not have both parents raising a child."

"So do I," she blurted, wondering if he planned to step in as a male role model for Kevin. "I mean, my mother died when I was young and my dad kind of went off the deep end. Last I heard, he's somewhere in Alaska. He left me with my grandfather when I was nine."

Zeke's dark expression hardened and softened all in one breath. "Let me guess. He promised to come back for you."

She nodded. "Yes."

"I got that, too. Jake and I...didn't know each other until we were older. I always admired him, wanted to be like him. But...we have different personalities, different codes on how to do things."

"I kind of gathered that you two were complete opposites," she replied. "Soup's ready."

She didn't miss that sizzle of awareness that seemed to purr around them like some exotic wind. Was she projecting her tumultuous feelings for Jake onto his brother? Or were her feelings for this honorable man the real deal? She didn't want to think beyond that. Zeke was way out of her league and...she'd learned her lesson with FBI agents. Too secretive and too driven.

Now that the adrenaline of trying to stay alive and find her missing son was draining down, Penny only wanted to curl up in a tiny ball and cry for a long time. But she steeled herself against that and glanced at Zeke.

"What?" he asked, his hand on a high-backed chair.

"Nothing." She'd been staring. Couldn't stop doing it. "I guess I'm just comparing you to him."

Disappointment flashed through his eyes. "Many people have. I always used to fall short."

"Used to. But now, you're the brother who's doing his job."

"I'm the brother who *has* to do his job. I don't have any choice."

She sank down and opened a bottle of water. "Just like you don't have any choice being here with us."

"I'm here for two reasons," he said, his spoon dropping into his soup with a soft splash. "One, you're in danger. And two, you're family now."

His eyes, so different from Jake's, held her. Penny felt a chill even though she felt too warm. "I haven't had a real family in a long time," she said, touched and wary at the same time.

"Me, either." He shrugged. "Like I said, my mother is still alive but I don't get to see her much. She'll love Kevin."

She'll love. As in the future. Would he take her son to see his mother? This was all too much to comprehend at this point.

So she tried to dissuade him with a bitter question. "Even though he's Jake's son?"

"In spite of him being Jake's son."

She let that settle, deciding to focus on the hot meal instead of the good-looking FBI agent. So she chewed on a cracker and kept one eye on her sleeping son.

Zeke fed Cheetah and gave him a chew toy. The obedient dog took his reward and curled up beside Kevin. Then Zeke went back to his soup, eating in a quick, efficient way that showed her he was used to eating alone and in the dark. Cheetah guarded her son without any wasted movements, his every move at attention.

They were both well trained.

It scared her to think where she'd be right now if they hadn't found her. Shivering, she stood, the image of Jake's anger and threatening moves hitting her like a cold slap to the face. She had to get as far away from him as she could.

And she had no business having such strange, intimate thoughts about his half brother. The best thing she could do once this was over would be to leave Montana and start a new life somewhere else. Somewhere away from secrets and lies and covert operations.

"Are you all right?" Zeke asked her, sincere concern in the question and something more in his eyes.

"I'm so tired." She never divulged things such as that. She didn't like admitting defeat. "And I don't mean physically tired, although I am that. I just want to have that life I always dreamed of. A pretty house near a meadow and a stream, the work that I love, and a chance to raise my sweet little boy. The whole white-picket-fence thing, I guess. A real home. A real life."

Zeke walked over to her and took her hand. "C'mon, you're going to get some rest."

She tried to pull away. "I've got to clean up the dishes."

"I'll do that. Go ready yourself for the night and I'll stand watch while you and Kevin rest."

Penny couldn't speak past the lump in her throat, so she hurried into the tiny bathroom across from the back storage room. The cold well water dripped onto her hands and she washed her face and cleaned herself up the best she could. Then she came back into the living room and saw that Zeke had moved Kevin to the bed and placed him up against the protection of the wall. He stood at the kitchen sink, but he wasn't washing dishes. Instead, he was staring out the tiny back window. Staring into the night.

"I'll want to know more," he said, without turning around. "I just need to know more about why my brother went rogue. And I'll need to know more about your relationship with him, too."

"Okay." She took off her hiking boots and dusted off her feet and crawled into the small bed beside her son, the warmth of his little body giving her hope. "Good night, Zeke. You'll know all you need to know about me soon enough."

"Good night," he said, his back still to her, his gaze lifting out into the darkness beyond the cabin.

Penny lay there watching him, wondering

what he must be thinking. Wondering how the anguish that wrapped around him like a dark mantle could ever be lifted.

He'd find Jake. She knew it. And when he did, he'd want answers from him, too.

Finally, she closed her eyes and prayed again. Over and over. But in the end, she wasn't sure what she should be praying for. Redemption, a reprieve or for all of them to simply survive this?

Or…for that little house by the meadow with the stream flowing nearby.

Alone, if need be. She could handle alone. She'd handled that feeling most of her life.

Or with a man who could love her son as his own.

Someone, but not the man standing watch over her tonight.

He didn't seem ready to be the loving kind.

EIGHT

Zeke hadn't slept much.

Every snap of a branch against the cabin jarred him awake and forced him to make rounds, Cheetah at his side. Every creak or groan from the old wood caused him to shift and reach for his Glock, his gaze always hitting the two people sleeping on the bed in the corner. He had to keep them safe. Somehow.

This was a strange twist in the already strange, twisted scope of this entire case. A little boy and a pretty woman. He'd somehow become their protector.

He'd come here to help find Jake, and for months now, that had been his goal. He'd never imagined he'd find Penny and her son again and certainly not like this, with Jake trying to kidnap them and take them out of the country. While he'd worked with the FBI Classified K-9 Unit to find Jake, he'd worried about Penny and her son. Jake's son. Now things had taken a more dangerous turn. Jake was back and determined. His brother wouldn't give up without a fight.

Now Zeke's goal had shifted. His first obligation was to protect them while he focused on finding his criminal half brother. So he stood there, watching the dawn lifting through the trees, and wondered what else he could do besides sit and watch. This work was so secretive, so classified, that he couldn't just blurt it all out to the world. He'd already told Penny more than she should know. But…the woman deserved some answers.

Over the last few months, he'd searched and researched to the point of exhaustion, but he couldn't find anything that would incriminate Penny. She couldn't be arrested for bad judgment and she seemed sincere in not knowing anything about what Jake had been doing. Besides…the man had tried to kill her. Because he wanted the boy? Or because she knew too much and he was afraid she'd spill it all? He hadn't seen anything in her words or manner to indicate that she wasn't telling the truth. But it was his job to question anyone connected to a suspect.

Zeke's gut told him she was innocent in all of this. He's seen the fear in her eyes when Jake had held her at gunpoint and when she'd realized her son had been taken. Even more than fear, he'd witnessed the complete agony of her realization that Kevin had been in that van.

"What are you doing?"

Zeke whirled to find Penny standing by the bathroom door, her hair disheveled and cascading around her face, her eyes sleep rimmed and full of questions.

"I'm thinking," he admitted. "We can't stay here forever. I need to get you to a safe house."

She moved toward him, the patter of her bare feet hitting the old wood with purpose. "I thought *this* was a safe house."

"Not really." He stalked past her to the old percolator-style coffeepot and poured some of the coffee he'd made earlier. "It's isolated but vulnerable. No security except Cheetah and me."

"You're the best. You showed me that yesterday." She took the coffee and stared into the steaming brew. "But you don't trust me, do you?"

"I don't trust many people."

Penny pushed at her hair and took a sip of the strong coffee. "But shouldn't you trust me? I've told you what I know but… I think you don't believe me. I understand why you wouldn't. I was close to Jake for a long time but… I can see him for what he is now. Any remaining loyalty I had for the man evaporated yesterday."

Zeke jumped on that one. "But before yesterday?"

She slammed her cup down so hard on the table, coffee splattered on the old wood. "Before yesterday, I was still too naive to see the truth. I ran from the truth and put my son at risk and now I'm paying for it. I wish I'd gone to the authorities when Jake contacted me and demanded that I leave with him. That would have been the smart thing to do. But..."

"But you held out hope, even when you were running?"

She sank down onto a rickety chair. "Yes. For my son's sake. I wanted him to know his father."

"No matter what?"

She looked confused, crushed, beaten. "In spite of it all, yes." Shrugging, she lowered her head. "I never had that as a child. I didn't want Kevin to suffer the way I had."

Zeke stopped grilling her and sat down to offer her an energy bar for breakfast. "I'm sorry he hurt you. But... I told you I wanted to know more. I'm trying to understand why he'd risk everything and give up a career he seemed to love. Why would he give up on a chance for a good life with you and Kevin?"

"That part should be obvious," she said, her head down but her eyes on Zeke. "He loves the thrill of the chase more than he loves his son and me. He's an adrenaline junkie. Aren't you all?"

Zeke took that in and shook his head. "So you don't trust me, either?"

"Why should I?"

"You sure are cranky in the morning."

She lifted her chin and gave him a haughty look. "I am, especially when an FBI agent is asking me too many questions before I've had enough coffee."

Zeke wanted to tell her she could trust him because he was trained to do his job, but mostly because he wasn't the type to allow a woman and her child to be in danger. But Kevin cried out and she immediately went to her son. Zeke would have to convince her that he was on her side or this could all go very bad.

And she'd have to show him she was on his side, too.

The day moved along at a slow pace that made Penny's skin crawl. She wasn't one to sit still for too long. She'd tried reading a book but Kevin was fussy so he demanded her attention. When she asked Zeke if they could go for a walk, he said no.

But he took Cheetah out. They scoured the woods and stayed close to the cabin, but she knew it was more than a bathroom break for the canine.

When they came back in, Zeke took Kevin in his arms and did the airplane thing, flying the little boy in the air while Cheetah watched in fascination but never uttered a bark. But late in the day, Kevin tired of play and began to fret again.

"He's confused and exhausted," she said, wishing she could ease her son's pain. "I have medicine in the diaper bag. I'll give him some of that. He's had some ear problems off and on, so he might be coming down with something."

"Maybe he's just tired, like you said," Zeke told her. "He had a traumatic day yesterday. Let me try rocking him."

After she gave Kevin the suggested amount of liquid pain medicine, Zeke took Kevin in his arms and sat down in the rickety old rocker where her grandfather had spent many hours.

Penny sat on the couch, watching. Her son took to Zeke without hesitation and listened aptly while Zeke told him all about Cheetah's heroic ways.

"Cheety," Kevin interrupted, clapping his hands. "Doggy. Woof."

Cheetah's ears lifted, his solemn eyes on

Kevin. Kevin poked at Zeke's solid chest. "Talk! Cheety!"

Zeke laughed and started back up, the animation in his words making him sound young and carefree. And irresistible.

Did her son see something in the man that she kept denying? Zeke rocked back and forth, steady and sure, Cheetah curled up nearby. The scene took her breath away but Penny closed her eyes to that sweet image.

After Kevin had fallen asleep, Zeke carried him to the bed and turned to stretch. "This is hard work, isn't it?"

She smiled and nodded, too overcome to speak. Then she swallowed back her emotions. "Yes. But the best work. I want so much for him. I don't know how to protect him and that scares me."

Zeke's gaze moved over her. "Well, for now, you don't need to worry about that. I'll be with you until we find Jake."

Kevin tossed and turned but he finally settled down for a couple of hours but woke around two in the morning. Penny gave him some more liquid medicine and Zeke walked the floor, holding him until he became drowsy again.

Penny watched Zeke with her son, her heart

bumping a warning that she was treading into dangerous emotional territory.

After Kevin drifted off again, they shared another power bar Zeke had fished out of his go-bag. "You're right," she finally told Zeke after they moved from the table to the couch. "It's hard for me to trust you even though you seem to care about Kevin a lot. But Jake brought us together, and now it's like walking through hot coals. He's here with us, a constant reminder of why we're together and in hiding. You know him as well or better than I do. I should be asking you all the questions."

"I told you, we weren't close until we were grown. I didn't see then that he resents me because of what our dad did to us. That's what drives him now, that need to find power and control. He's not thinking straight, out to kill all of us just to get even. He had a lot of pent-up anger and bitterness inside him, a lot more than anyone realized. I could have helped him, talked to him, if he'd been willing to let me."

Penny decided Zeke needed to talk. So she listened to him and responded back in reassuring tones. A tentative honesty developed between them and they laughed and told each other childhood stories that held some good memories before they moved on to future hopes, well into the night. It was almost easy for her to forget that they were hiding out from a man who wanted to kill both of them. A man whom they'd both loved. After Zeke had painted an overall grim picture of his life and how for a brief time he and Jake had grown closer, he finally confided, "And now…everything's changed. I don't want to track my own half brother but… I have to do my job."

Penny understood that concept. "He's throwing away his life for greed and money."

"Yep. I think he's pretty much committed a few of the seven deadly sins."

"But you're different. You're solid."

"I'm not perfect," Zeke said, staring over at Kevin. "But I have faith that everything works toward the good."

"And yet, you fight the bad."

"I have to. I want justice."

"Is that because of your dad leaving you and your mom?" she asked.

Zeke's frown told her this turn made him uncomfortable. "No. His leaving only made me want revenge. I wasn't sure what kind of revenge, but I wanted someone to pay."

"But you chose justice instead."

He nodded. "My mom insisted I attend youth meetings at the local church where we lived in Utah. I didn't want to, but… I found my strength there. I had people willing to guide me and help me. Stand-ins for my dad, but good people. My faith is solid because of that."

It gave her comfort that he felt the same way she did. That he loved Christ and turned to the Lord in his times of need.

"You're a good person, Zeke."

He shrugged that compliment off. "I want to help people. I want the bad guys off the streets."

"It must be so hard, chasing after Jake." She'd seen his anguish, his pain, in that standoff yesterday.

"More than I can ever say."

They sat, silent, sleepy, and let this quiet bond form between them. Penny felt the wall around her heart tumbling away, little by little.

"It's almost dawn," he finally said, his voice low and husky. "You should try to rest."

Penny nodded, yawned and stood up.

A sound echoed out over the warm night. A shot rang out, shattering the window behind them.

Zeke threw her back onto the couch and shielded her with his body, his heart racing right alongside her own. Cheetah stood and woofed low.

"Are you all right?" he whispered, his breath warm on her earlobe.

She managed a nod and heard her son's soft cries. "Kevin."

Zeke sat up. Cheetah danced around, eager to get going. Zeke put a finger to his lips, gave Cheetah the quiet command, and went for his assault weapon.

"Stay with Kevin," he said. Then he pushed a hand through her hair and held her eye to eye and handed her his Glock. "I mean it, Penny. Do not leave this cabin."

Penny nodded, her heart trying to beat again. She might have thought about running on her own yesterday, but not now. She had to trust Zeke enough to keep Kevin safe at least.

He turned the kerosene lamp off and darkness surrounded them. A quiet hush settled around the cabin. Then another sound. Stomping through the woods. Footsteps coming closer.

Zeke motioned to Penny. "Get down."

She slid down on the couch but didn't stay there. Instead she did a quick crawl toward her sleeping son. Kevin whimpered, "Mommy." Carefully putting the gun down on the floor, she scrambled up on the bed. When she touched him, his skin was burning hot.

Fever.

Penny glanced toward where Zeke crouched by the front window, listening. Cheetah stood by his side. Someone was out there. Kevin stirred and coughed. Zeke glanced back, his finger to his lips again. Penny eased up onto the bed and stroked Kevin's forehead. His skin sizzled with a burning fire.

When footsteps sounded just outside the door, Zeke pressed against the wall. "Don't move, Penny," he whispered. "Understand?"

She nodded and waited. Zeke lifted up into a crouch and gave Cheetah a silent command. In one swift move, both man and animal opened the front door and pounced. One shooting and the other barking.

That commotion brought Kevin fully awake. "Mommy!"

He started sobbing and she took him in her arms and tried to soothe him. Hearing gunfire, Penny closed her eyes. Praying. Hoping. Holding her breath.

Silence followed. A deadly silence.

Dear God, protect us, please. Protect my son.

She prayed for Zeke and Cheetah and thanked the Lord for providing them to protect her and Kevin. She'd never doubt Zeke again. She only prayed he'd come back through the door at any minute now.

As dawn began to seep through the undergrowth and the sun's first rays shot off the jagged rocks like a golden laser, Zeke called the canine back. "Good job, Cheetah," he said, rubbing the eager animal's head. "We nipped at 'em good, didn't we, boy?"

He'd seen the dark figure lurking near a big pine about fifteen feet from the cottage. And he'd purposely shot into the air near the tree to scare whoever it was and maybe flush them out. A hiker or camper would have identified themselves and probably would have taken off. However, this person hid, quiet and waiting.

Until Cheetah began to growl and alert right near the tree, which meant the Australian shepherd had picked up a hostile scent. Gunther Caprice, who tried to take Kevin? Or was Jake crouching behind that tree?

"You can come out now," Zeke said in a low whisper. "Or I let my partner bring you down. He can bite through your leg and make you bleed out in about ten seconds."

When he heard heavy footsteps running away, he had his answer. Someone knew they were here. That meant more would show up. He could go after the runner but he couldn't risk leaving Penny and Kevin for too long. He'd kept one eye on the cabin the whole time.

He hurried back inside. "We have to go. Right now."

Penny got up to stare over at him, her eyes

filled with dread. "Zeke, Kevin has a fever. And I don't have enough medicine left to contain it. We have to get him to a doctor."

Not the best news right now, but the boy had to come first.

"Okay. We need to leave and I promise I'll find him some help."

They loaded up their few things and hurried to where he'd hidden the SUV. Zeke looked around and spotted footprints. Heavy boots. Then what looked like tire marks from a possible off-road vehicle.

"They've found us," he said as they got into the vehicle. "They'll be back with reinforcements. But...their scout also knows I saw him."

"Did you try to kill him?" Penny asked, her words tight with dread.

"No. I shot at him once and tried to wait him out. I wanted to question him. But he ran away."

"Why didn't you call for help or go after him?"

"No reception and I didn't want to leave you and Kevin alone."

She slumped against the seat and stared at the woods. "You could do your job if you didn't have to worry about us. You had to let Jake go for our sake and now this. Your boss is going to get tired of that excuse."

"It's not an excuse, Penny. I am doing what I think is right for you. I told Max that I was staying close to you two and right now, he'll have to deal with that. He's out there working the scenes and searching for Jake and anyone else who's been wreaking havoc. We all want to bring in Jake and his hit man."

"I shouldn't be complaining," Penny said with a pensive sigh. "Not after yesterday. I want this over. It's hard not to want that."

"We're on the same page there," Zeke retorted.

He maneuvered the massive vehicle along the rutted dirt lane. "Once we're out on the main highway, I'm calling Max to tell him we need to move you to a secure location."

"How does Jake keep finding us?" she asked, a tremor in the question.

"I don't know," he admitted. "GPS? Or maybe…someone on the inside giving him clues."

"Is that possible?"

He shot her a grim glance. "With my brother, anything is possible."

NINE

They were halfway to the road when Zeke spotted two ATVs motoring through the trees, two men dressed in camouflage and armed with guns and bows and arrows. He couldn't make out if the two were Jake and Gunther, but he figured they'd both be somewhere calling the shots by now. These two looked as if they knew these woods and were prepared for a hunt, but he doubted that even if it was the early bow season.

"They're still here," he said, pointing up ahead to where the men were steering into the woods around a bend. "Two of them now."

Zeke slowed and turned off behind some heavy brush and scattered boulders. "Let's wait them out."

He knew he could take down the men on the four-wheelers but his first concern had to be his two passengers. If he got shot, Penny would be exposed and taken. Or worse.

This dilemma only added to Zeke's woes. Bad enough that he was up against his own brother and Jake had managed to get away, even worse that right now, Zeke was the only one who could protect Jake's ex-girlfriend and his son.

Zeke didn't want to think about how Max West would react when he finally called in. *Not positively, that's for sure.* But…he had to go with his gut and Max would just have to do what he had to do.

He watched as the ATVs moved on up the path and took off on another trail. Breathing a sigh of relief, Zeke knew they had to get out of these woods.

They waited a few more minutes, but Kevin was fussing and pulling at his right ear.

"I think this is another bad ear infection," Penny said, worrying clear in her eyes. "We have to get him to a doctor right away."

"Once we're out of here," Zeke said.

They made it to within a few yards of a row of cabins located just off the main road. Zeke figured the people looking for them would stay away from the more congested areas to avoid anyone seeing them. He was about to turn and take a back way out when a man came running out of the woods and tried to flag him down.

"Careful," he said to Penny. "This could be

a setup." He pulled his Glock out of his shoulder holster, just in case.

But when he spotted a frantic woman and young girl with the man, he let down the driver's-side window and waited. "Can we help you?"

"Yes," the woman said, pushing past the man. "We were hiking and when we turned around, our nine-year-old son was gone. We don't know what happened. Have you seen a little blond-headed boy anywhere?"

"No. Have you called the authorities?" Zeke asked.

"We've tried. The reception is horrible and we can't get through to the ranger's station. We need help now. The other cabins are empty. You're the first people we've seen."

Zeke glanced over at Penny. He needed to get her and Kevin out of here, but he couldn't leave a family in need.

"I know," she said, wariness in her words. "You have to try and find him."

"I can search for your son," Zeke said. "But I need to get a physical description and a scent from some of his clothing so I can let my dog help me track him. He's good at that."

The frightened parents bobbed their heads and then the dad said, "Whatever you need. But hurry, please. He likes to sneak away and play hide-and-seek and we've warned him about not doing that. We're worried about him being attacked." The frantic man waved his hand in the air. "I mean, we know the dangers—bears, elk and antelope, mountain lions. We've called and called and he's not answering."

"Show us your cabin," Zeke said. "We have a sick little boy and we can't linger here too long."

"Whatever you can do," the man replied. "We'll keep trying the ranger's station, too."

The man's shocked expression and nervous pacing proved believable. But people could be convincing when they were desperate.

"Thank you. We're here." The woman pointed to a cabin sitting up on a hill. "Right over there. We thought maybe he'd come back here but he's not inside."

Zeke followed the hurrying parents and parked the SUV close to the small cabin before turning to Penny. Whispering low, he said, "We're married and we were at another cabin for two nights. Our son got sick so we had to leave. Our *family* dog is good at tracking. That's all they need to know."

"I could assist you in the search," she said, nodding. "But I can't leave Kevin."

"I'm not sure I should leave you two with them. We'll check out the cabin and decide."

They made it into the cabin and the parents, Brian and Marcy Wilder, gave him a picture of their son, Cody. His older sister, Jessica, looked as frightened as her mother.

"Okay," Zeke said after they'd brought him a T-shirt. "Here's the deal. My…wife and son need to stay here while I conduct the search. I need all of you to stay put. If you go out on your own and get lost, it could hamper me finding your son, understand?"

"We understand," Marcy said. "Just hurry, please. He has asthma. I'm so afraid he'll have an attack."

"He has his inhaler," Jessica said, trying to help.

Zeke took it all in, his gut burning with instincts he'd honed over the years. Hard to say who was telling the truth. But he had to find the boy before he stumbled upon a wild animal or those two men roaming around.

Then he turned to Cheetah. "Let me do a quick search here in the cabin first. That will help my dog to pick up Cody's scent, too." He gave Penny a warning glance, hoping she wouldn't blurt out anything about him and Cheetah.

After he finished a sweep of the cabin, he

nodded to Penny. "Stay here and give Kevin the last of the drops, okay?"

"We have medicine," Marcy offered. "Over-the-counter liquid. Cody has a hard time taking pills."

"Thank you," Penny said, glancing toward Kevin. "He has a fever. I think his ears are bothering him."

"We have a thermometer, too." Marcy buzzed with nervous energy while she gathered what Penny needed.

"I'm going," Zeke said to Penny. On a low note, he added, "Don't let anyone into this cabin. Do what you have to do. Use any weapon you can find. If I don't come back soon or if someone threatens you, take the SUV and leave."

"I won't leave you," she replied, that determination he'd seen the first day they'd met shining through.

"You will, to keep Kevin safe," he whispered. "I can take care of myself."

Realization overshadowed her stubbornness. "Okay."

"Good. Now, I need to get a plan going."

"Zeke, I have an idea," she said. She turned to the couple. "I'm a nature guide so I know most of this area. Did you pack walkie-talkies or two-way radios?"

"Yes." Brian hurried to a battered desk and grabbed a duffel bag. "We didn't use them this morning because we were only going on one last short hike before we headed back to Salt Lake City."

"Okay." She took one and handed the other one to Zeke. "I can guide you," she said. "We can stay in touch."

"Good idea," Zeke replied, admiration in his words. "And you can use it if you need me."

Penny glanced around the small room. "We need a map."

Brian found one. "Here's ours. It's one of those easy maps." He was right. The map was colorful and animated and included trailheads and mile markers. He showed Zeke and Penny the spot on the trail where Cody had disappeared not far from the cabin.

Zeke gave a curt nod. "I'll start there and see where Cheetah takes us."

"Are you trained for this or something?" Brian asked Zeke.

"We're just careful when we're out here camping or hiking," Zeke replied. "Since my wife works out here and knows the dangers."

"Let the man go," Marcy said, the urgency in her words heartbreaking.

Zeke gave Penny one last glance then headed out with Cheetah. He only prayed that the boy hadn't been taken by the men lurking about on the ATVs. If Jake had to kidnap another child to get his own back, he'd do it in a heartbeat.

And that would turn into a worst-case scenario.

Once they were on the search, Cheetah took off toward the trail where they'd spotted the men on the four-wheelers. Could they have already taken Cody? Zeke hoped not. Giving Cheetah the quiet signal by dropping his hand down firmly, he allowed the dog to lead him along the path. They stopped several times so Zeke could check the tire marks in the rutted lane and search for footprints. When he didn't see two sets of footprints, one big and one small, he breathed a sigh of relief. But it was hard to find solid prints in the dry dirt.

Then Cheetah alerted and emitted a low growl as they were moving through a cluster of evergreens. Zeke stopped and heard voices up ahead.

"He said an old cabin, away from the others. I'm telling you, the one we found last night has to be it."

"But he wants the boy. That cabin looked deserted when we went back."

"Somebody shot at you last night, remember? Someone with a trained dog."

"Yeah, and now that somebody is gone. The cabin is empty."

Gunther? He'd run away yesterday when he heard Cheetah growling, according to what Penny had told Zeke.

"We shoulda gone in last night," his friend said on a jerky whine.

"Not me," Gunther retorted. "He's not paying me enough to get eaten alive by a trained police dog. I don't like dogs, man. I'm not taking any chances." Cheetah glanced up at Zeke, apparently taking in that information for future use. *Good for you, boy.*

The other man sounded off again. "Look, let's find the kid and get out of here. We heard a kid crying. They have to be hiding somewhere around here. Boss wants that kid, bad. And as for the rest, well, that's why we brought all these cool weapons, right?"

Zeke heard stomping, followed by two motors revving to life. He watched from the shelter of the trees as the two ATVs took off toward the main trail out of the woods.

What if they found the wrong boy?

"C'mon, Cheetah," he said, giving his dog the go order. "We gotta hurry, buddy."

Cheetah took him deeper into the woods but back toward the circle of cabins. When Cheetah alerted near a small ravine about a hundred yards from the cabins and turned back to face his handler, Zeke glanced down and saw a stream below. And something else.

A little boy, curled up in the fetal position.

Penny checked Kevin's forehead again.

"How's he doing?" Marcy asked, her expression filled with worry.

"I think his fever is going down but I'm afraid his ear problems aren't going to get better until I get him to a doctor."

Marcy nodded, her brown eyes misting over. "Cody's always had allergies and when we realized he had asthma, I didn't know what to do. But we've learned how to deal with it."

She held a hand to her mouth. "I should have been watching him more closely."

"Hey, you're doing the best you can," Penny said, understanding the woman's fears. "We can't always be there to protect them."

"I… I just want him back with me," Marcy said, tears falling. "I have to pray that your husband will find him. God sent you two at exactly the right moment."

Penny hugged Marcy close and prayed for her. But the woman made sense. God had certainly sent Zeke to her at just the right time and now this. Maybe there was a greater purpose in all of this. If she hadn't met Jake, she wouldn't have her beautiful little boy. But her bad judgment had brought consequences.

And maybe redemption.

Zeke was a good man. She felt that at this moment with all her heart. He'd do his best to find Cody and he'd protect Kevin. Zeke had turned toward the right path, rather than choosing a life of crime and destruction. Remembering how earlier he'd called her his wife and Kevin his son, Penny tried to ignore the punch of longing in her heart.

"You're right," she said to Marcy. "God's timing is always perfect, no matter the outcome."

"But sometimes the outcome is bad," Jessica said, bursting into tears. "Sometimes God doesn't help."

Both women looked up at the girl. "Oh, honey." Marcy rushed to her daughter's side. "It's all right. It'll be all right."

"I teased him, Mom. This morning. I dared him to go into the woods."

Marcy gasped and stared down at her daughter. "Why would you do that?"

"I was mad at him for messing up some of my sketches. I'm sorry. I didn't think he'd run away."

Brian came over to stare at his daughter.

Penny held her breath, wishing she didn't have to witness this.

But he took his daughter into his arms and held her close. "It's okay, sweetheart. Your brother can be a handful but…this man Zeke seems to know what he's doing, right?"

He glanced at Penny, hope in his eyes and a certain understanding that showed he wasn't going to ask any more questions. He just wanted his son back.

Penny knew that horror. Had lived it since Jake had taken her along that path. She needed to stop questioning Zeke, too. Maybe if she gave up being problematic and unyielding, she might remember some detail that could help them.

She stood and brushed her hands down her jeans. "He does know what he's doing so we have to trust him."

Brian nodded and patted Jessica's back. "We'll talk about the rest later. After your brother is safe again."

The walkie-talkie on the table crackled with static. Penny grabbed it and held it tight while the anxious family waited to hear.

"I've found him," Zeke said into the walkie-talkie. "Copy?"

"Ten-four," Penny replied, her throat constricting. "Is he okay?"

The family gasped and rushed toward her, Marcy and Jessica crying, Brian looking anxious. She held up a finger, warning them to wait.

Zeke's voice cracked through the static. "Yes, he's calling out to us. But I can't get to him. He's down in a ravine by a stream."

Her heart constricted with fear but Penny tried to stay focused. "Describe the area. What's your location?"

Zeke called off the coordinates. "We're about a half mile off the main trail leading out to the highway on the left by a heavy cluster of evergreens." He described some nearby trail signs and the surrounding rocky hills. "We're near the direction sign for the ten-mile hike."

"I'm looking at the map," Penny reported back, her mind going over what she remembered about this area. "I think there's another way down to the ravine." She told him about a little-known path that followed the water. "It should be a few yards south of where you're describing."

"Thank you," Zeke reported back. "Keep everyone there until I can report in. I might need some help."

"Copy," she said. "Over and out."

She turned to Marcy and Brian. "He's okay

but we have to stay here unless he calls us. It's too dangerous."

"I want to see him," Marcy insisted, turning to her husband. "Brian, let's go."

"We have to listen to Zeke," Penny told her, thinking about the dangerous men who could be lurking in those woods. "Marcy, let him handle this. He'll report back in when he has Cody safely out of that ravine."

"What if he can't bring him out?" Brian asked.

"Then he'll call us to come and help."

"I'm going to find them," he said, heading for the door.

"Brian, stop." Penny rushed toward him. "Listen, we saw what looked like some hunters in the woods earlier. It's too risky since bow-hunting season is open for antelope right now. Remember, Zeke told us he can't help Cody if he has to stop and find one of us out there."

Brian frowned over at her. "So we just wait and worry?"

She had to word this very carefully. "For now. We can't get any outside help so Zeke is doing everything he can." She gave Cody's parents a sympathetic look. "Zeke knows what he's doing and it's best we don't distract him."

She only prayed that would be enough, and

she *really* hoped Zeke didn't run into any of Jake's men while he was out there trying to save that little boy.

TEN

"Cody, can you hear me?"

Zeke called out again, listening as the boy's sobs became clearer. Remembering the boy had asthma, Zeke hurried down the slippery rocks near the splashing stream, Cheetah rushing ahead.

"Hey, buddy. Are you okay?"

The boy wouldn't speak. Then Zeke saw him curled up shivering and holding himself tightly, as if he were trying to melt into the rocks and brush.

"Cody, your parents sent me. I'm going to help you."

The boy's scared voice echoed out over the woods. "I'm not supposed to talk to strangers."

Zeke couldn't identify himself as a law officer since his work was classified, and he was already pushing the envelope by even attempting to help this family.

"That's right. You're doing fine. But I've

spoken with your parents. My name's Zeke and I brought my dog, Cheetah, with me. He's really good at finding people who are lost."

Cody raised his head, his eyes red rimmed and wide. "Is he a good dog?"

"The best," Zeke said, stepping an inch or two closer. "He really likes kids. He knows not to bite someone who needs help. And you look like you could use some help."

"I lost my inhaler," Cody whimpered. "And I don't feel so good."

Not great news, but Zeke could work around it. "All right, buddy, well, the sooner you let me help, the sooner we can get you back with your parents. Meantime, take deep, slow breaths."

Cody started unfolding his bruised, scratched legs and stretched them out. "Okay. So you're not one of those scary guys?"

Zeke's blood went cold but he hurried toward the boy. "Did you see some scary guys?"

Cody was sitting up now. He wiped at his eyes and bobbed his head, his breath coming in shallow gulps. "Yeah. I hid from my stupid sister but I got lost and… I heard them saying they had to find the boy and they sounded mad. I ran away and I fell, then I ran again and I heard water running and Daddy always says to follow the stream."

"Your dad sounds real smart," Zeke said, his

gaze sweeping the woods. The wind whistled and moved through the lush pines and leafy aspen trees that towered over them, blocking out the late-summer sun. In spite of the warm day, he was concerned that Cody could go into shock. Or have a full-on asthma attack.

So those goons had been nearby when the kid darted away. They'd probably heard Cody calling for his parents. Zeke sent up a prayer of thanks that Cody had been smart enough to hide and that the two on the ATVs had left the area.

Cody stared at Cheetah. "I've never seen a dog like that. He's all different colors."

Keep him talking. Zeke hadn't dealt with children a lot since his work was mostly about capturing criminals, but he knew if he kept the kid engaged, things would go better. Thinking of the time he'd spent with Kevin, he had to admit he'd love to have a kid.

Zeke smiled and squatted by the boy. "Cheetah is an Australian shepherd. But his breed actually got started in the American West, during the gold rush. You've probably heard all about that in school, huh?"

"Nope. But my dad talks to me a lot about stuff like that. He's a professor. He sure didn't know about this dog, though. I'll have to tell him."

The kid's breathing was leveling off.

"Okay, well, Cheetah is a special kind of dog. Most people don't know much about him, but his breed is also a good family dog. He's part of my family because I've helped train him to be a working dog. He's going to help me get you back to your parents. First, I need to check you over. Do you hurt anywhere?"

Cody nodded. "I fell and skinned my knees. And my arm hurts."

Zeke looked at his left arm. His wrist was purple and swollen.

"Mind if I touch that spot?"

Cody shook his head.

Zeke pressed the swollen wrist and the boy winced. "That hurts real bad."

"You might have a twisted wrist or…it could be broken."

Which meant he needed to get the child out of here, and soon. Shock could definitely set in and if the bone was broken, it would need to be set as soon as possible.

Cheetah stood guard but Zeke noticed the dog's ears lifting. Then he heard a grinding motor nearby.

Not good. The last thing he needed right now was a run-in with two criminals. Looking around, he figured they could hide here but the boy needed medical attention. He'd have to take his chances on getting Cody out of here.

"Okay, Cody, we're gonna take you to your folks. I'm going to lift you up, okay?"

The kid looked afraid. "Are you really going to take me to Mom and Dad? Am I in trouble?"

"I'm going to get you back to them and, no, you're not in trouble."

Slowly, he lifted the shaking boy. "You've been very smart and brave. Cheetah is impressed."

The boy stared down at the dog. Cheetah's curious stare seemed to satisfy him.

Zeke heard motors purring up on the trail. Trouble on the way.

"Is that someone else coming?" the boy asked, his eyes wide. "What if it's those mean men?"

"You let me worry about that," Zeke said. He didn't want to get in a shoot-out in front of the kid.

"Guard," he commanded to Cheetah. The dog would give his life to save them but Zeke hoped it wouldn't come to that.

He took the rock trail that followed the stream, but going uphill was tougher with the boy in his arms.

"I can walk, you know," Cody said.

"I have no doubt about that, but I got you, buddy."

Zeke would shield the kid if things got serious.

When the roaring motors grew louder, Zeke knew their time was running out. He couldn't let those men see him with this boy.

Penny held the two-way radio with an iron grip, wishing she knew what was going on. Already, she'd heard the hum of some off-road vehicles moving through the forest.

Marcy and Brian paced and whispered, holding each other's hands anxiously.

Kevin was asleep in one of the bedrooms, within sight.

And Jessica was sitting by the window, waiting and watching.

Penny went to her but took a seat where she could still keep a watchful eye on Kevin. "It's not your fault, you know. Brothers and sisters torment each other all the time."

Jessica wiped at her eyes. "He's such a pain but… I love him."

"Yes, he'll always be a pain. Brothers are made that way." She thought about the two very different brothers who were both now entrenched in her life. "But as long as you love him, you can forgive him."

Could Zeke do that with Jake? Would Jake bother to forgive Zeke for doing his job? And how was she supposed to forgive and forget after these last few traumatic days?

"Will he forgive me?" Jessica asked, a fragile hope in her pretty blue eyes. "And Mom and Dad? Will they forgive me?"

"Of course." Penny smiled at her. "When he gets back, he'll be so happy to see you he'll probably forget why he hid in the first place. And I'm pretty sure your parents have already forgiven you."

She only prayed that whoever was driving around out there wouldn't stand in the way of Zeke getting Cody back to his family.

Dear Lord, please help this family. Keep Zeke and Cody safe. Protect all of us.

Then they heard a crackle over the walkie-talkie.

"Come in," she said while the room went still. "Zeke, can you hear me?"

"We're on our way back," he replied. "Pack up and be ready to go. And tell the Wilders to be ready to move, too. Cody might have a broken arm."

She knew what that meant. Those guys were either chasing him or they were too close for comfort.

"Over and out," she said, turning to face Cody's parents. "Your son is safe and on his way here but he has an injured arm. You need to be ready to leave immediately."

They held each other and cried tears of relief then went into a frenzy of finishing up what little packing and cleaning they had left to do.

Jessica stood by Penny, hesitating.

When her mom turned and held her arms open, the girl rushed into her embrace.

Penny couldn't help but get all misty-eyed. She was tired and frightened and worried. Tattered and torn. She had to hold out hope that Zeke would get her and Kevin to a doctor and then to a safe house where they could all rest.

If he could only make it back here first.

Zeke held Cody against him, careful not to crush the boy's injured arm. "Keep that wrist up and close to your chest," he instructed. "You're doing great."

Cheetah scouted ahead, stopping now and then with his snout in the air. The slightest hint of a familiar scent and he'd alert them. Zeke came around a copse of aspens cluttered together in a thick symmetry. The ATVs had moved on for now, but those men could show up again at any minute.

When he heard a rustling in the woods behind him, Zeke ducked into some tall grasses and signaled for Cheetah to come. Then he put a finger to Cody's mouth. "Shhh."

The little boy clung to him and stayed silent. Someone was moving through the dirt and jutting rocks just below them.

Zeke held his breath and settled Cody against a tree, careful to shield the boy. "I'm right here," he said in a low whisper. "I'm not leaving you."

Cody bobbed his head.

Zeke took out his handgun from underneath the waistband of his pants. The boy's eyes went big but he didn't say a word.

The noise grew closer. Right below them now.

Zeke crouched in front of the child while Cheetah stood, protecting Cody on the left. They all waited, not moving, with insects buzzing around them like hungry wolves.

Then Zeke saw it. A magnificent male elk that looked to weigh about seven hundred pounds. The bull elk lifted his head, his antlers shooting out like a regal crown. He was establishing his domain. Which meant he'd picked up their scent.

"Wow," Cody said in an exhaled breath of a whisper.

"*Wow* is right," Zeke replied in the same awestruck whisper. "We'll let him pass."

"Can he hurt us?"

"Only if we provoke him."

Cheetah's ears stood straight up but the dog did his job and stayed still. They stayed quiet, watching the massive animal until he finally lowered his head and strolled away.

When that bit of excitement was over, Zeke waited several minutes before they started moving again. They were within sight of the cabin when he heard motors roaring to life behind them on the trail.

"Cody, hold on tight and protect your wrist," Zeke said. "We're gonna make a run for it."

With that, he signaled Cheetah to trot ahead. Zeke took off through the woods, the sound of gunshots firing all around them.

Penny heard the gunshots and rushed to a window.

"What's going on?" Marcy asked in alarm. "You said you saw some hunters earlier. Bow hunters."

"They had guns, too," Penny explained.

"But they shouldn't be shooting," Brian pointed out. "Not at this time of year."

"I know." She turned to them and said, "Once you get Cody back, I suggest you load up and get out of here. It's not safe."

Brian stared at her. "So…you're not talking about normal hunters, are you?"

"No," she admitted. "I don't know who they are, but they scared us enough that we're leaving. You should, too."

Before Brian could question her further, the door burst open and Zeke came barreling in with Cody in his arms and Cheetah on his heels.

"He has a possible sprained or broken wrist," Zeke said, handing Cody off to his dad. "A few scrapes and bruises but other than that, he seems fine."

Marcy and Brian fussed over Cody while Zeke turned to Penny. "Let's go."

She didn't argue. Turning to Marcy, she said, "There's a clinic up on the main highway into Iris Rock. On the left. Take him there."

"But…"

"We have to go," she said, wishing she could say more. She hurried into the bedroom and scooped Kevin into her arms.

When she came back, Zeke was already headed to the door. But he turned to face the Wilders. "You have a very brave son. He should be fine."

Zeke gave Cody a thumbs-up sign and the

boy grinned. "Thanks, Mr. Zeke. We got to see an elk."

"We sure did, buddy. And you were a real trouper."

"We can't thank you enough," Brian said. "Is there any way we can help you two?"

Something passed between the two men. Brian had figured out Zeke was more than just a nature lover with a good guard dog.

"Yes," Zeke said. "Get out of here and…pretend you never saw us."

With that, he urged Penny out and into the waiting SUV.

"Thank you," Jessica called. "For saving my brother."

Zeke nodded and Penny gave the girl an encouraging smile. Then Zeke got in and started the vehicle.

The Wilders followed, carrying luggage and storage bags. They hurried into their own vehicle, Marcy holding Cody in her arms.

And not a minute too soon.

The men on the four-wheelers whirled around the curve and spotted the two vehicles leaving. They gave chase but Zeke made sure the Wilders were well on their way before he fired a couple of shots out the driver's-side window, blowing out a tire on one of the ATVs and hitting the fuel tank of the other one.

Those two weren't going anywhere for a while.

When they were on the main road, he turned to Penny. "First, I'll call Max and report in. Then we wait to hear where I move you next. And I'll get someone we can trust to come and check on Kevin's ear infection, I promise."

She bobbed her head. "Okay. How bad did things get back there?"

"Bad enough," he admitted. "An elk stalking through the woods and those two searching all around us. I'm so thankful I got Cody out of there. He could have died in that ravine or…they could have found him and used him for leverage."

"I'm glad, too," she said. "I hope they make it home safely."

"They will," he reassured her, his official phone in his hand. "Max will make sure of that when I give him the Wilders' license plate and ETA at the clinic."

"You think of everything," she said.

Zeke shrugged. "I've been trained to think of everything."

"Zeke?"

He glanced over at her, weariness cloaking him now that the adrenaline was dying down.

"Thank you."

Zeke smiled at the gratitude in her pretty eyes. "Yes, ma'am."

Then he hit the number for Max West and waited for the fallout.

ELEVEN

"Are you all settled in?"

Penny whirled from her spot at the kitchen counter, still shell-shocked. "Yes, thank you," she said in response to Zeke's question. "This place is definitely an improvement over my grandfather's cabin."

The handsome agent stood across the room near the empty fireplace. The new safe house was about thirty miles north of Billings in a spot on a hill with open valleys and rocks below. She should feel safe here and she did feel much better after a shower, a good night's sleep and a solid breakfast this morning. But she couldn't help but worry.

Zeke tried to reassure her. "Yes. Secluded, gated and posted with no-trespassing signs. Nothing out of the ordinary last night, thankfully."

She wondered when this man ever slept. He

and Cheetah had prowled around last night like two crouching lions, always on the hunt.

Penny poured two cups of coffee. "Well, we are surrounded by officers with dogs."

Zeke took the coffee she offered, his dark gaze washing over her with all kinds of mixed emotions. "I can't be with you 24/7, so the team is stepping in."

Max West had stepped in all right. She knew from listening and watching Zeke's stoic expression that he'd received a royal dressing down for taking matters into his own hands. "You took a risk, hiding me like that. I'm sorry your boss isn't happy."

"Technically he's not *my* boss, but for now he's the man in charge. I insisted on joining the hunt when I realized the Dupree family had taken my brother."

"Or so you thought at the time."

He nodded and glanced over his shoulder. "I was also concerned about you."

That was a new revelation. Giving him a shocked look, she said, "I thought you only became worried about me when you found Jake holding a gun on me, what, two days ago?"

"I worried long before that." He told her about asking special permission to help with the search. "At the time, I was apprehensive about all three of you, but I told Max and the team about you and Kevin. I had a hunch Jake would try to contact you."

"Why?" she asked. "Did you think I would help him? Hide him?"

"I wasn't sure," he admitted on a gruff tone. "Mostly, I wanted to make sure you were both safe. I went with my gut and I was right."

Penny didn't press him. They'd talked a lot back at the cabin but he hadn't mentioned this at all. He couldn't tell her very much due to the classified aspects of his job, but she'd pieced things together enough to know he came here to help track down his brother but discovered the horrible truth. The same truth she'd had to accept.

Jake had willingly gone with Angus Dupree that day all those months ago. How long had he been playing all of them?

Penny dropped that topic since it made her broken heart throb painfully. "I wish I could just walk out of here and keep going."

"But you know that's not safe, so don't do anything that could cause you or Kevin more harm."

She'd already done too many stupid things, so his warning was unnecessary. Right now, however, she felt safe and sound and secure. As secure as she could feel under the circumstances.

The house was lovely. Rustic and solid, it sat

up on a hill, which held a stunning view of the mountains and valleys all around. It wasn't too big. Just two bedrooms and a huge kitchen and living room area with a massive stone fireplace and glass windows lining one wall.

She'd been told to stay away from those windows.

"How bad are things with you and the boss?"

"Not so bad," he replied, shrugging. "I've been in worse trouble."

"But I heard him telling you that you couldn't go dark on him again. Does that mean what I think it means?"

"It means next time I take you away, I have to stay in touch." He took a long swig of coffee. "They knew we were together but they didn't know our location. Meantime, they've checked all along the basin. Jake might be long gone but he's still got people out there. The two thugs who came after us stayed well hidden until they thought they had us. Now apparently they're the ones who've gone dark. Right along with my brother."

Penny's insides went cold thinking about how close they'd come to getting into a battle with those two henchmen.

"Well, we're here now, and we have guards," she said, trying to find the good in this. "I don't see us going anywhere soon. In fact, I think your team is watching us as much as they're watching for Jake and his goons."

"They're friendlies," he replied. "You've got Nina Atkins coming next with her Rottweiler, Sam. She'll help me with the next twelve-hour shift."

"Is her dog safe? I mean, around Kevin?"

"He's trained to do as he's told. He won't harm your son. Most Rottweilers can be safe if handled and trained correctly. Trust me, Sam is a pro." Zeke drained his coffee. "How's Kevin doing?"

"He's much better. Thank you for finding a doctor."

"We have our ways," he replied with a heart-stopping grin. "So the antibiotics are helping?"

"Yes, but the doctor said he might have to get tubes in his ears to finally clear things up for good."

"There is so much that goes into caring for a child." He settled into a deep, cushy leather chair by the fireplace. "I never realized how much. I admire how you always put him first."

"I love him. He's my life," Penny admitted, wondering if he was thinking of his own single mother. "I'll do what I need to do to protect him."

"When this is over," Zeke said on a measured note, his gaze capturing hers, "I'd like to be a part of his life."

"When this is over, you'll head back to Utah, won't you?"

His dark eyes flooded with indecision. "I might not. I don't know yet."

Penny sank down on an ottoman across from him. Kevin was asleep in a pop-up crib in the guest bedroom right next to this room, the door open so she could see him and Cheetah. The dog seemed to know his duty was to protect her son.

She didn't know how to respond to Zeke's surprising uncertainty. What would *she* do after this was over? If this was ever over?

Here they were, forced together again, in a nice house with a breathtaking view. She could almost pretend that her life could be like this. Except that each time she glanced outside from her corner of this luxury prison, she saw armed people with canines walking the perimeter.

"What if this is never over?" she asked, fear in the one question and an image of always looking over her shoulder cluttering her mind. Jake could stay hidden for years. He had the means and the motivation to do whatever he wanted.

Zeke did a sweep of the room. They were alone. He got up and came to sit next to her on the cushy ottoman, the masculine warmth radiating from him giving her strength. And causing her to wish for things she couldn't have.

When he took her hand in his, Penny almost pulled away. He'd never touched her like this before. It thrilled her and frightened her. She didn't dare fall for Jake's half brother. It wouldn't be right. It couldn't work. But her hammering heart was having trouble accepting that fact.

"It will be over," he said, his fingers covering hers. "The outcome isn't going to be good, either way. But it will end. The team combed the basin and woods and those men are gone but they left a lot of evidence behind. They're searching for the make and model of the ATVs, hoping it will lead them to a tip. They managed to preserve some tire tracks and they found some casings but those could both be from other people."

"They might not ever find those men," she said, desperation coloring her tone. "Jake always did know how to cover his tracks."

Zeke held tight to her hand. "I gave a detailed report on what transpired, including us helping the Wilders. And I told the team that the men sounded aggravated and on edge. They keep getting thwarted and to a criminal, nothing is more frustrating. Sooner or later, they will mess up big-time or they'll grow tired and turn tail and run, leaving Jake and his bribes behind."

She'd given up but his words reassured her. Maybe those men would figure things out and decide it wasn't worth it. "So until then, I stay here?"

"You stay where I stay," he said, the look in his eyes going from professional to intensely personal.

The air between them hummed with an awareness that had little to do with an FBI agent keeping her safe. Penny tried to shake it off but her attraction to Zeke was overwhelming and hard to explain. He made her feel things she'd never felt before—security, respect and a newfound hope. So she tried to ignore the way he leaned in as if he wanted to kiss her.

When they heard a door opening, Zeke stood abruptly and turned to see Max West moving into the room from the main hallway, his all-seeing gaze hitting on their guilty expressions.

Putting down a box marked Petrov's Bakery, he motioned to Zeke. "A word with you, Agent Morrow."

Zeke winked at Penny and moved over to the kitchen with Max. "Sir?"

"What's going on here?"

"Um… I'm guarding a woman in danger?"

"Yeah, we've all figured that one out," Max said, his icy stare burning a hole in Zeke's brain. "Fraternizing?"

"Sir, I…"

Max actually cracked what might have been a grin. "I'm messing with you, but with a warning. Be sure of what you're feeling. Things have been crazy over the last few days and you're all mixed up in this because someone you care about is in a heap of trouble. Don't mistake fatigue and adrenaline for something else."

"You've been through this," Zeke pointed out, chafing underneath Max's burning assumption. "A lot of the team has. How did you handle it?"

"Not very well at first," Max admitted, referring to how he fell in love with and married Katerina Garwood, a woman who'd once been engaged to a drug trafficker involved with the Dupree family. "And I don't have any right to fuss at you since there seems to be a wedding in the works with every month that passes. It's just…you're close to everyone involved in this case."

"You mean my half brother and his ex-girlfriend and my nephew, Kevin?"

"Isn't that enough? You can't protect all of them. You're going to have to make some tough choices from here on out."

"No, sir, no choice," Zeke replied. "I'm doing my job." He shrugged. "And while I'd like to bring Jake in alive, I'll do whatever it takes to end this once and for all."

Max let out a grunt. "I'm going to believe you haven't been deliberately letting your brother and his cronies get away. Instead, your first priority is protecting the boy and his mother, right?"

"You can take that to the bank, sir," Zeke replied. "I couldn't very well leave them in the woods to fend for themselves. So, yes, I made the decision to stay close to them instead of pursuing any and all threats. I counted on my team to cover me on that."

Max gave him a hard-edged glare but he didn't dispute Zeke. "Okay, Zeke, I get it. So far, nothing from the basin area and most of the tips we've received haven't panned out. I think even though you had two people stalking you in the basin, Jake has pulled back or maybe left Montana. But make no mistake. He's hired underlings to finish the job and he'll still come after the boy even if he's not physically around to do it himself."

Zeke nodded brusquely. "He'll keep coming. He's just trying to figure out where we are."

"I don't know how he's finding you. We couldn't even locate you out there."

Zeke ignored Max's pointed comment. He didn't know how Jake managed, either. But he had the techs on it. "Dylan is checking for anything suspicious. Jake could have someone on the inside watching our every move."

Tech guru Dylan O'Leary worked tirelessly behind the scenes to uncover anything on the Duprees or Jake Morrow. He was good at digging up data where no data was supposed to be found.

"Are you accusing someone on my team, Agent Morrow?"

"No, but I'm saying Jake is smart and he had a lot of people fooled. He knows people on both sides of the law and he can be very persuasive."

Max looked skeptical but finally nodded. "He does seem to slip through our fingers at every turn."

"Maybe someone should talk to Violetta again. Did she go back to Chicago?"

"Yes, but she should be back for Reginald's trial, whenever that might be." Max rubbed his scar. "Soon, I hope. Ian and Esme will be able to come back to the States once this is over."

Agent Ian Slade and Esme Dupree had gotten married and immediately went into the witness protection program until this was all over. Esme's brother, Reginald, might be in jail, but he could still put out a hit on both of them.

"I can't wait that long," Zeke said, hoping he'd be able to attend that trial. Max's frustration over both only mirrored his own.

With Reginald in jail and Angus dead, the whole organization had become fractured. The FBI had been rounding up underlings all over the country. But Jake still remained at large and now they had a bead on Gunther Caprice, too. He'd been a thorn in their sides since he'd slipped away before all the fireworks started. He probably knew where all the bodies were buried so why had he come back to help Jake? Did Zeke's brother have something on him?

"I want this over," he said, glancing toward where Penny sat reading a magazine. "Violetta showed up in Florida and shot Angus. She had a way of keeping tabs on her brothers and it makes sense she's doing the same with Jake."

"Why don't you ask Penny some more questions?" Max suggested, his expression blank. "She's only one of a long line of women who've been involved with Jake. We've questioned several of them and they all describe Jake's habits and MO the same as she has, but she might remember something none of the others can." Max pivoted his head toward Penny. "Because of the boy."

"She doesn't know anything," Zeke replied, anger fueling each word. "We've all questioned her. I think she just got caught up with the wrong man."

Max put his hands on his hips. "I'll get in touch with Violetta and see if she has any inkling about Jake's current movements or past deeds. Meantime, you do what you're here to do. Protect Penny and her son. And bring down your half brother."

"Yep, there is that." Zeke gave Max a long stare, wondering if the man still doubted his loyalty. "Something else has been niggling at my brain."

Max's eyebrows shot up. "And…?"

"Dylan keeps me up-to-date on a lot of things and one of them is how concerned he is about Zara. They can't even communicate now. She's not responding to his texts or emails."

Zara was Dylan's fiancée but she was in training at Quantico and should be home in time for their fall wedding. If everything went according to plan. But something was up at Quantico. And that bothered Zeke. Zara had gone into training around the time Jake had disappeared with Angus. That, and Dylan's concerns, caused a nagging worry in Zeke's mind. If Dylan couldn't find out what was going on, no one could.

Max pulled out his sunglasses. "Yes, we're all concerned but Quantico is in charge of Quantico and Zara Fielding knows what to do. She's there to learn. That's what recruits do. We have our own case to worry about."

"What if the two are connected?" Zeke said. "What if Jake is involved somehow?"

Max looked confused, his piercing blue gaze filled with resolve. "Do you think he's got someone on the inside at Quantico?"

"Anything is possible with my brother," Zeke said. "Penny did make one remark about him going on and on about Quantico once when he called her. About all the people depending on him, all the people he trusted. But he told her he couldn't trust them anymore."

"We all have friends who've been through Quantico, Zeke, and not all of them stay friends. What's your point?"

Zeke shrugged again. "She said he sounded off, scattered and unsure. Jake could have someone there watching and listening and maybe that person is willing to help him. And he has to know Zara is training there. He could be trying to distract Dylan so he can't dig too deep into Jake's case or…he could have someone watching Zara and hacking into her personal messages."

He took a breath and rushed ahead. "Zara wouldn't talk about *our* case. But another agent could give her the wrong intel just to throw her off, thinking to mess up our whole operation. We're a highly classified unit, Max. Jake's known for creating distractions to cover his tracks. He did that this week when he held Penny and let Gunther kidnap Kevin."

Max studied Penny then pinned Zeke with a stare. "Did Dylan put this weird theory in your head?"

Zeke shook his head. Dylan planned to investigate as much as he could, but Max didn't need to know that right now. "No, but I've been taking notes and trying to figure things out. The timeline fits. Dylan's been concerned since Zara left right about the time Jake went rogue on us. He could be trying to get just enough information to stalk out our whole case."

Max shook his head. "It's a long shot because we didn't even know Jake had turned until months later. All Dylan knows is that Zara's class has had some trouble. You need to leave it at that."

"Jake had already turned when we thought he'd been kidnapped. He probably started covering his tracks the minute he took off with Angus in that chopper." He tapped his fingers on the kitchen counter. "I'm hoping Dylan will prove me wrong but I'm not letting this go until I know what's behind it. Besides, we owe it to Dylan and Zara to stick our noses into this, don't you think?"

Max didn't argue with that. "This is far-fetched, Zeke. But I guess it's worth looking into since we don't have much to go on in the first place. Jake knows a lot of people at Quantico and if he convinced someone he's been wronged, they could be trying to dig up information on our every move to report back to him. That would explain how he's always one step ahead of us."

"And Gunther Caprice is helping him. Gunther could still have connections, inside and out. Another thing to consider."

They talked a few more minutes before Max left. The day passed slowly but Zeke did insist that Penny should get some rest, so he took over with Kevin for a while. He enjoyed feeding the little boy and playing games with him. Kevin loved it when Zeke grabbed his stuffed horse and made whinnying noises.

They were playing that game when Zeke looked up to find Penny standing at the bedroom door wearing clean jeans and a black sweater, her damp hair like dark liquid gold, her eyes full of both hope and trepidation. He saw the gentle longing in her eyes. It tugged at the emptiness inside him.

Kevin giggled and pointed at Zeke, bringing him back to the present. He kept trying to say Zeke's name but it came out as "'Eke."

"'Eke? Horsey?"

Both Zeke and the boy giggled. Even Cheetah seemed to be in on the joke. But Penny's smile froze on her face. The longing in her eyes turned to a wariness that left Zeke cold.

She still wasn't sure she wanted him in their lives. So he watched her take Kevin for his bath and bedtime then waited for her to come back to have dinner with him.

While he waited, he wished for so many things and told himself with each wish that he couldn't have those things. His father had been a womanizer and now his brother was a criminal.

What did that make him?

Penny came back into the living room and gave him a weak smile. "You wore him out. That's a first." Then she motioned to the kitchen, her smile gone. "Let's eat."

A man could get used to this, he thought later as the sun began to set over the mountains. They had a quick dinner of sandwiches and soup but didn't talk much, mostly because Kevin woke up again, full of energy, which didn't allow for any personal talk. Which was maybe for the best.

Penny had become distant and wary again, so she must have had the same doubts as he did. Had he gone too far in playing with Kevin and helping to take care of him?

He was about to delve into that question when Nina Atkins arrived with her K-9 partner, Sam, and went over the routine with Zeke. She'd done a good job guarding the Wild Iris so Max had rotated her around to helping Zeke. He'd put Timothy Ramsey on the inn. Another good rookie. His dog, Frodo, specialized in arson detection but they could both handle any situation.

"We have locals down by the gate and you and me up here inside the house," Zeke said, updating Nina. "I just need to grab a few winks. We can take turns."

"Grab a lot of winks," Nina replied, her short blond hair falling in spikey waves around her temples and chin. "Sam and I don't mind staying up. We're night owls."

"So is our subject," Zeke said, glancing at Penny. She'd rooted herself into a cozy chair pushed up inside the only corner without windows, probably because it was right next to the bedroom where Kevin was sleeping. Or maybe because she'd tried to avoid Zeke for the last few hours, too.

Something had almost happened earlier there on the ottoman. He'd wanted to pull Penny into his arms and kiss her. Which would only make matters worse. He was here to do a job, to find his brother and maybe spare Jake's life at least. It wouldn't be a good life. He'd be behind bars for a long time. But if there was a chance…

Then what? You take over as Daddy to his son? Bring his son to see him in prison?

Zeke turned back to Nina. "I think I do need to get some rest so I can get my head straight."

Nina nodded in understanding. "I'll go and introduce myself to Penny and let Sam and her get acclimated to each other. Where's the boy?"

"Asleep in a crib in the second bedroom. We hope. He keeps waking up." Zeke pointed to the room with the curtains drawn and a single lamp burning. "He's been through a lot."

"I'll take care of them, Zeke," Nina said. "Sam won't let you down."

"I'm not concerned about you and Sam. You're a good agent," Zeke said. "I just hope *I* don't let Penny and Kevin down."

Then he turned and headed for the other

bedroom so he could get a shower and catch some shut-eye. But he had a feeling he wouldn't be able to sleep. If Max, and now Nina, had noticed the closeness he and Penny were feeling, then everyone else would soon see it, too. He couldn't let his personal feelings cloud his judgment, though.

Zeke couldn't deny that his feelings for Penny had changed over the last forty-eight hours but it was way too soon—and too dangerous—to decide what those feelings could mean.

TWELVE

Penny heard the gunshots at the same time Cheetah started barking. Then the night turned chaotic. Zeke hurried into her room, barefooted. He carried his weapon and wore a black T-shirt and jeans. Kevin sat up and started sobbing.

"Get down on the floor," Zeke said, not waiting for her to reach her child. Instead, he lifted Kevin out of the crib and, crouching, passed the child to Penny. "Stay here and stay down."

He turned to Cheetah and ordered, "Stay. Guard."

Cheetah went silent and stood alert in front of Penny and Kevin, his body pointed toward the door.

"I'll be back as soon as I can," Zeke said before he hurried through the house. "Nina and Sam are right here."

Penny held her son and soothed his tears while she tried to stay strong. Cheetah became the consummate professional. The dog seemed to be frozen in stone in front of where she'd pulled Kevin to a dark corner by a chunky nightstand. Cheetah kept his snout in the air and his head toward the open door. Having been protected by the amazing canine before, Penny tried to stay calm.

Glancing around, Penny searched for anything she could use as a weapon. When she saw a set of black bookends enclosing three classic novels, she grabbed one and held it close. The heavy metal shaped like a ladder gave her a sense of confidence but her rapidly beating heart and the cold sweat trickling down her body reinforced her fears for her child.

She'd fight anyone to the death to save Kevin. Even his own father.

Zeke rushed through the house and out the door, shouting to Nina, "Don't leave them alone."

The rookie agent, who'd been sitting with a view of the front yard, had already jumped into action. She had her weapon out and Sam was leashed and roaming around the big den. "I saw at least two out there, Zeke. They split apart. Be careful."

"Roger," he called.

Zeke made it out the front door in a low crouch, his bare feet hitting the rocky walkway in a silent thump, cold wind rushing over him. He heard more gunfire, barking dogs and voices echoing out over the yard. When a dark figure whirled toward him and fired, just missing his head, Zeke fired back and the man slumped to the ground.

Then silence.

It was all over in a matter of minutes.

Zeke held his gun on the figure sprawled out on the walkway. Then he leaned down and felt the man's thick neck for a pulse. He was dead.

Leo Gallagher and his Labrador retriever, True, who'd been patrolling outside, trotted up. "They were trying to get to Kevin. I heard them talking. 'Kill anyone but the kid,' one of them said. 'Keep the kid alive.'"

Zeke stared down at the man on the ground. "This one isn't going to talk. What about the others? Was one of them Gunther?"

"Hard to say. The one I saw was dressed all in black, including a mask, and he ran down the hill. I've got someone searching for him and the other one."

"Everyone accounted for?"

"Yes, we're all good," Leo replied. "I'll take care of things out here."

Zeke nodded and turned toward the house,

relief rushing over him in great waves. "I'm going to check on our subjects."

When he got inside, he found Nina standing guard with Sam inside the den. The dog roamed around, sniffing and listening. While Sam specialized in cadaver detection, the animal could also take down a criminal in about zero seconds flat.

"We're all safe," Nina said, glancing toward the bedroom.

He nodded. "All clear outside, too." Then he went to the open bedroom door and called out. "Penny, it's Zeke. Everything is under control."

She didn't move from the corner.

He called Cheetah. "Come."

Cheetah hurried toward him but Penny stayed in the corner, holding her son with her left arm around Kevin and a metal object in her right hand. When he kneeled down in front of her, she lifted her head to stare into his eyes, a stricken expression on her lovely face. "Nothing in my life is ever going to be under control again."

Zeke couldn't get through to her. She was done. Penny was slowly giving up, that spunk he'd so admired in her turning into a sputtering spark that was about to fizzle out. He had to try and keep her going. They had to move again.

So he went back into the corner where she sat in the big chair, holding Kevin asleep in her arms.

Outside, dawn shimmered through the tall conifers, the sun's rays shooting against the rocky hills in a brilliant announcement of the new day.

"Penny, I know you're tired. We all are. But we have to keep moving." They should have left hours ago but she'd held on to Kevin and refused to move. "We've been compromised. We have to go."

"No," she said. "I'm not moving my son again. Unless it's to a place far away from Montana. I can't do it, Zeke. I'm tired of hiding in dark corners. And I can't be around you anymore. Every time I look at you, I think of Jake."

That angry comment floored Zeke. She'd never want anything to do with him even if he did catch the bad guy. Because she was probably still in love with Jake, and she was right. Being around Zeke only reminded her of all that she'd been through with his brother. Zeke didn't know how to deal with that kind of pain. He sure didn't know how to make her see that he could never do the things Jake had done, that he'd never intentionally hurt her. But he could hurt her in so many other ways if he didn't play this right.

He stood and scratched at his five-o'clock shadow. Giving Nina a blank stare, he headed to the kitchen for some coffee. They'd ID'd the dead man as Claude Baxter, formerly from Chicago. He had a record and he'd first been hired as a bouncer at a well-known bar owned by the Dupree family and moved on to join the ranks of the Dupree crime syndicate. Since that family was officially busted up now, Jake had to have taken over paying the man's salary. Apparently, he was bribing or blackmailing people to do his dirty work.

The other intruders had managed to escape in spite of canines searching all night long. The trail had gone cold down on the road. They must have hopped into a getaway vehicle and taken off for parts unknown. The team was searching for reports on stolen or carjacked vehicles in the area. So far, nothing.

Nina came to stand beside him, her dark brown eyes full of sympathy. "I can talk to her."

"Have at it. I'm at about the end of my rope."

Nina poured a cup of the fresh coffee and headed to the corner. Penny hadn't eaten any breakfast yet, but then neither had he. Someone had opened the muffins and pastries Max had left, but the thought of eating turned Zeke's stomach sour.

This had to end. Jake had some kind of hold on them and if he knew his brother, he also had spies everywhere. How else was he constantly finding them?

He hurt for Penny and Kevin. He mourned his brother's lost logic and lack of decency. What could he do?

He could pray, and he had prayed, over and over. Zeke thought about calling his mother, but he tried to leave her out of his work problems and since he couldn't explain what was going on, he refrained from doing that. But he wondered if Jake would try to contact her as a last resort. She'd call him if that happened. His mother had been a newshound since she knew a little about his work. She would have heard about Jake by now.

The world knew about him but he seemed to be hiding from all of them. Now Zeke had to wonder if he could ever get Penny to a truly safe place.

Then something hit him square in the gut. Whirling so fast he surprised Cheetah, Zeke headed for the corner where Nina sat talking to Penny. "I need to go through that bag you carry around," he said to Penny.

"You mean Kevin's diaper bag?" she asked, clearly shocked at the strange request.

"Yes. That and your backpack, too. Where are they?"

Nina gave him a questioning glance. "In the bedroom. I'll get them for you, Penny."

When Nina hurried away, Penny stared up at him. "I told you and I just told Nina, I want to go back to the Wild Iris Inn. I'll get the rest of my stuff. Maybe I'll buy a plane ticket to Florida. Or maybe California. Or… Canada."

"Just hold that thought," Zeke said, grabbing the colorful bags Nina brought to him.

When he dumped the contents of the diaper bag out on the big ottoman by the chair, Penny glared at him. "What are you doing, Zeke?"

"Looking for a GPS tracker," he said. "I think I've figured out how Jake keeps finding us."

Penny couldn't believe she hadn't known about the tiny metal tracking device that Jake had embedded inside the plush lining of Kevin's favorite stuffed animal. He'd had it sewn in so deeply, they would have never discovered it. A small slit in the horse's underbelly had been resewn with tight brown threads but Zeke had pressed his fingers all along the seam and after finding a pair of scissors, had opened the stitches.

After digging his fingers around, he had pulled out a small cylinder that wasn't much bigger than a dime. "It looks like a key fob," he said. "He'd have to be nearby to locate you, but it's doable. This is made to track pets within a certain radius but Jake's smart enough to have something state-of-the-art inside this thing."

"He sent that to Kevin right before he disappeared," she said, gasping. "He must have figured this would happen."

"He wanted to get back here and take his son," Zeke replied. "So he planned ahead. He must have driven all around the basin area before the inn showed up on his tracking device, probably his cell phone."

Then he held up the other one he'd found in her backpack. "He could have easily dropped this one inside your backpack when he took you the other day."

"He's been tracking me all this time," Penny said in a weak whisper after she'd put Kevin in his crib. "First the stuffed animal and now the backpack."

"Yes. If he wanted to keep tabs on you, this was a good way to do it without anyone knowing." He pointed to the diaper bag. "He put one in the toy to mainly keep tabs on Kevin, but he wanted to keep track of you, too. So he could distract you long enough for Caprice to take the boy."

She put a hand to her mouth and held up her backpack. "He's been watching us since the beginning! He was coming for me in Colorado but I got away."

Zeke let out a grunt. "He's had a bead on you for months now. That works much like a GPS. No cameras or recordings, just a little dot on the map he can follow on any electronic device. He lost you for a while there, so staying on the move was smart on your part, but he must have asked around and found out you were back working as a wilderness guide." A muscle ticked in his jaw. "He distracted you so the man could get to Kevin. The stuffed horse has been with us since then along with your backpack, and that's how he found you at the cabin and here."

"That and his ability to dig up enough info to hunt us," he added. "Jake can charm anyone into giving him information."

"And now?" she asked, getting up to pace the room. "Now you've disabled both of those things?"

"We have," he said, his tone grim. "But we have to save the trackers and the stuffed horse for evidence."

"Now Kevin loses his favorite toy, too?"

"I'm sorry," Zeke said. "I'll find him another one."

Penny rubbed her hands up and down her arms to get rid of the invasiveness that covered her. "And that will make up for everything, right?"

She hated the hurt she saw in his eyes. Wishing she could take back her careless comment, she lowered her head. "I'm sorry, but I can't believe this. Jake's been spying on me. I can't hide from that."

"Just another sign of how far he's willing to go to get his way," Zeke said, his voice husky with regret.

A shiver moved down Penny's body. She felt violated and exposed. And hurt. How could Jake do something like that?

Because he'd lost his soul through greed and bitterness and a need to…to what? Prove himself, brag about his dirty money? To give his son all the things he'd never had?

She whirled, dizziness overtaking her. "I can't—"

Zeke was there, holding her up, getting her to the sofa and into the beautiful midmorning light that she'd tried to stay away from. "Sit here," he said gently, his eyes holding hers.

Penny sank down. "Kevin?"

"Cheetah is guarding Kevin."

Zeke looked down at her, his dark gaze washing her in that same brilliant light. "I know this isn't easy."

"No," she said, "it isn't, and I shouldn't take it all out on you. I'm sorry for what I said earlier."

His expression changed. She could see the war within his soul. Then he sank down beside her and pulled her into his arms. "I can make you forget him, Penny."

She gasped, tears misting her eyes. Deep down she wanted that. Wished for it with every fiber of her being. "But Kevin is his son."

Zeke glanced around. They were alone, and that attraction pulling at them proved impossible to resist. He lowered his head and kissed her, a gentle brush of their lips that deepened for only a couple of seconds.

And burned through her soul.

Then he pulled away and stared down at her, the light in his eyes softening. "Kevin needs me in his life. And… I'm beginning to think I need both of you in my life."

She stood, running a hand through her tousled hair. "I can't do this now, Zeke. It's too much, too soon. You don't know me and I don't really know you. I can't risk it."

Zeke stood, too, and took her hand. "I know.

We'll wait and see how this goes. We can't do anything until we find Jake. And after that..."

After that, they might not want to be anywhere near each other. Ever again. No matter what happened, the shadow of Jake's horrible downfall would haunt them.

"He's going to die, isn't he?" she asked. "They're going to kill him. You'll do it if you have to, right?"

Zeke's eyes turned dark and grim. "I'll do my job, yes. And right now, that means I'll get to anyone who tries to hurt you and Kevin."

"Is that it? Your sense of protectiveness has kicked in? Or is it more of a sense of taking down the older brother who betrayed you?"

"Penny..."

She saw the frustration in his eyes, saw that torment that had carried such weight with both of them. "Jake will always be there between us, Zeke. Whether he's dead or alive. And we'll both always wonder, won't we? We'll wonder about him and...we'll never quite trust each other."

She turned, wishing she hadn't hurt him, wishing for so many things that could never be. But the wall around her heart ached with a heaviness that would never go away. She'd believed Jake loved her. Finally. After her mother's death and her father's abandonment, finally, someone besides her precious grandfather loved her.

But she'd been fooled and abandoned yet again. And so had her child. So she couldn't trust herself to fall for Zeke. Not now. Not so soon after Jake's lies and deceptions. Her exboyfriend had stood between Zeke and her from the start, and he'd always be right here with them.

"This could never work," she whispered. "I need to remember why I'm here. My son has to come first."

"He does come first," Zeke said. "From the moment I knew you had a son, I wanted to put Kevin first."

There was that about him, too. That need to do the right thing when everything was going wrong. Penny had to trust Zeke for now. She didn't have anywhere else to turn. And... hadn't she thanked God over and over for sending him to her? Why fight it when the urgency of the situation demanded that *she* needed to do the right thing, too?

"Get me out of here," she finally said. "The sooner we move on, the sooner this can be over."

When she looked back, she saw the stark resolve in Zeke's eyes. "You're right. I want this over as much as you do. And the sooner the better. Just prepare yourself. This is not going to end well no matter what we'd each like to believe."

Penny kept walking toward the bedroom, the whisper of his gentle kiss still warming her lips. Did he believe that she still wanted Jake, after all of this?

That was a question that clamored silently between them.

And one she'd have to answer truthfully sooner or later.

THIRTEEN

Another remote cabin. Another stunning view.

Penny stood away from the reinforced windows but the mountains and valleys still stretched before her in the last throes of summer. Soon the leaves on the aspen and cottonwood trees would change and the tamarack conifers would turn golden and drop their fronds. These woods would change from burning orange, brown and gold to stark grays and whites, covered in snow. She'd been told these windows allowed those inside to see out, but no one could see inside. A special tinted and reinforced glass that allowed for privacy and yet showed off this amazing view.

A prison nonetheless.

She missed being free. Being out there in the fresh air and the wind. She missed so many things that she promised herself she'd never take for granted again once she was allowed to be on her own. If she ever got to go outside again. But she wasn't sure she'd ever feel safe in the woods after this experience.

"My whole life has been put on hold," she said, turning to where Zeke sat scrolling on his phone. "I hope Claire and Rex are okay. I've had them on my mind, too."

"We've got people watching out for them," Zeke replied. "Nina told me they're doing great. Rex said he wasn't going back to Florida until he knew you and Kevin were safe."

Penny smiled at that. "He's a widower who decided to travel the country after his wife died three years ago. He helps out around the inn. I miss Claire and Rex so much."

"Well, you'll get to see both of them again soon."

Penny hoped she'd see her friends again. But she knew Jake wouldn't want to leave any witnesses to testify against him. She'd brought this danger to the quaint inn she loved so much.

And yet here, she was surrounded by the best possible security team. Today, she and Zeke were alone in the cabin with Kevin while the rest of the team worked to follow leads and do whatever else they had to do to track down a wanted man.

But they weren't really alone. There were guards outside, waiting and watching, stalking around with loaded weapons.

This house was sixty miles west of Billings and centered high up on a rocky hillside. While it was clean and held all the modern amenities, it still reminded her of her grandfather's cabin. It wasn't very big but it was solid, more of a good hunting cabin than a vacation retreat. Someone from the FBI owned it, so it had been custom built for protection if needed.

The home consisted of one large room with a massive stone fireplace along one wall, a huge kitchen and dining area and a den, all with floor-to-ceiling windows, and doors leading out to a sprawling deck. One big bedroom with an arched open doorway along with a bath finished out the other side and offered another stunning view of a small lake below.

Lovely. She could imagine being here on a retreat, resting and having a romantic time. A fire in the fireplace, soft music in the background, holding hands with someone she loved while the snow surrounded the whole place.

But Zeke had gone over an escape route with her, just in case things went wrong. That sobering discussion came back to her full force now. The small mudroom hidden behind the pantry off the kitchen, with an enclosed set of stairs leading out to a path down the hillside, was her way out.

She was beginning to hate cabins.

"How long is this going to go on, Zeke?" she asked.

"I'm trying to get any information I can," Zeke finally replied. "But all the tips we've received on Jake's recent whereabouts keep running cold. Sightings here and there followed by nothing. The man is trained to blend in and he knows how and where to hide. We've taken down one of his hired assassins but the others have managed to get away. No one has managed to get a bead on Jake since the day he tried to take you and Kevin."

"He knows how to disappear," she pointed out. But then, that was obvious. "He could have finally given up and left the country without us."

She hoped Jake had taken off so she could get back to some sort of normalcy. But that shoot-out last night proved it was probably just wishful thinking.

Kevin walked up to her and smiled, his chubby finger pointing to the window. "Bears."

"Yes, bears," Penny replied softly. She didn't want him to be afraid of the many animals that roamed the state, but bears had been the only logical reason she could give him for not going outside. "They play here sometimes."

"Play, Mommy. Outside?" Kevin ran to

Zeke, his big dark eyes hopeful. "'Eke? Outside? Cheety?"

Zeke's gaze collided with hers and caused a sizzling awareness to burn like a wildfire between them. She saw the rawness edging his eyes. "I wish we could, buddy, but—"

"Let's play with the blocks," she suggested, taking Kevin's hand to lead him to a toy chest they'd found in a corner. Sitting on the floor, she adjusted the jeans and big sweatshirt Nina had brought her earlier and took the wooden logs out and faked a grin for her son's sake. "Build Mommy a cabin."

Kevin went to work, his efforts a bit wobbly but his smile as bright as the sunshine. At least he was feeling better now.

Penny loved him with such intensity, it took her breath away. How could she protect him? Thankful for Zeke and his team, she turned toward the man.

Zeke glanced up, his gaze holding her, the look in his eyes telling her what she couldn't deny. He was taking this protection duty very seriously, but he'd shown her signs of tenderness and understanding. The kind of signs a woman could interpret as attraction. She couldn't put much store into what could never be.

Or did she dare to dream?

She'd given up trying to deny her attraction to Zeke, but at least now she knew she truly did like him and that she wasn't projecting what she'd felt for Jake onto his younger half brother.

This was different. Secure and strong. Faith filled and warm with hope.

Did he feel the same way? As if his whole world had shifted and changed, the terrain rocky and unsure but beautiful, as if his heart had begun to mend itself piece by piece with each tumbling step. Or did he feel the fear and doubt that plagued her each time she looked at him? That kind of emotional tug of a warning mixed with an anticipation that shouted "He's different but don't make the same mistake again."

She managed a weak smile. He nodded and looked as if he wanted to say more.

Then his phone dinged and he stopped to read something. "Dylan got a match for the ATVs' tire tracks. A dealer in Billings sold two ATVs that match the ones we saw to a big muscled man with a distinctive accent."

Penny grinned at Kevin while her pulse increased. "That looks great, honey. Build Mommy a pretty house, okay?"

Kevin grinned and held up a connecting log. "'Kay."

Penny kissed her son's chubby cheek then hurried to Zeke. "Could that be the man you shot the other night?"

"Sounds like one and the same," Zeke replied grimly. "I never got a good look at his face when we were in the woods the other day, but I saw him up close the other night and I'm pretty sure he was one of the two driving around on one of the off-road vehicles. Dylan's going to send out his picture to see if the ATV store manager can identify him as Claude Baxter."

"How will this help?"

"Well, if we can trace that man's movements, we might find Jake. Or at least start a trail and keep it going. We need to somehow connect Jake to this man. We have Jake's blood as evidence, too, from where Cheetah took a bite out of him."

"It's at least something to go on," she said, a little tickle of hope moving up her spine when she remembered that horrible day. He'd shared information he wasn't supposed to share and she appreciated knowing. But that hope was overshadowed by what might come next.

Zeke put his phone down and stood up, relief softening his rugged features. "This is major, a good lead at last. We're gonna celebrate this small step forward tonight since Dylan is doing all the footwork and reporting to Max, too. I have two new guards hidden on the property—local hires who are trained for this type of work. And the whole team scattered from the road to the woods all around us." He released a breath. "Jake is smart. He'll send someone else if he finds us but if we can snare one of his henchmen and get that one to talk, we'll turn a corner on this."

Penny glanced at Kevin still playing with his logs. Cheetah lay nearby, his alert gaze on her son. "I do feel safer here. The one big room with the adjoining open bedroom and the reinforced tinted windows all help."

"That and the new security measures. Plus, this place isn't even on the map. No GPS can find it."

"Right. And we've checked for those kinds of devices." She shook her head, remembering how they'd taken her phone and gone through the diaper bag and her backpack, even their clothes and the SUV, doing what Zeke called a full sweep. "Okay, I'll try to relax."

At least she had a big, good-looking man sitting at the table in front of her. "I'll cook something."

"No. I'm cooking. I make a mean chili."

"You cook?"

Zeke's grin wiped away the strain he'd been

under and made him look younger. Her breath seemed to leave her body. She couldn't even think about this—them together in a secluded cabin, enjoying a meal. Kevin safe and playing with the family dog. Life in such a sweet shade of gold, a too-bright gold that sparkled like the potted mums sitting on the front porch.

"Yes, I cook," Zeke replied. "My mom worked a lot of long hours as a hotel desk clerk and she still works part-time. I've had to fend for myself a lot."

She sank down beside him. "Tell me more about your mom."

"Deidre Morrow," he said while he went about pulling out frozen hamburger meat and all the ingredients he needed for the chili. "She's petite but powerful. She's tough but… I know she's also lonely, but she's happy for the most part. She taught me to keep going no matter what, and that's what she does. She has a good network of friends in Utah. A little town with a nice church, so she's always busy. But I miss her. I can't tell her what I do but she knows I'm in law enforcement."

"I can see those traits you mentioned in you," Penny replied as she went about chopping onions and peppers. Keeping busy and being normal did calm her shattered nerves.

"I'm tenacious," he admitted. He stirred the

onions and peppers, the smell of spices filling the air. Then he looked at her with those mysterious dark eyes. "I don't do things halfway. I became a cop as soon as I could get through training then worked my way up to the K-9 Unit in Salt Lake City. Transferred to the FBI and trained at Quantico. Worked for Homeland Security until I came here and…took Jake's place." He paused, his eyes searching her face. "I thought temporarily but now… I don't know how long I'll be here."

Penny felt the heat of his questioning appraisal all the way to her toes. Did his decision to stay or go depend on her? To hide her confusion, she hurriedly microwaved the meat to thaw it then helped him toss it into the big pot. He took a wooden spoon and broke it down, his precise actions belying the quizzical expression on his face.

She decided to stay on a safe topic. "Wow. You do work fast. Did you follow in Jake's footsteps or did you always want to be in law enforcement?"

"A little of both, I think," he answered, a trace of disappointment shadowing his face. "Jake decided early on he wanted to be a cop, even after he got into some trouble for petty crimes, since he had a relative who worked the beat and helped him out of some jams. But he went all FBI after the Bureau took over a local case and solved the murder of one of his best friends. Some kind of drive-by shooting." Shrugging, he added, "Maybe he never got over that murder. It hit him pretty hard."

Zeke stared at the steaming stew in front of him. "As for me, I watched a lot of cop shows when my mom was at work and, like Jake, I wanted to be a cop. I guess I did try to follow in our dad's footsteps since I admired him and looked up to him." He cleared his throat. "Our father was a businessman and a lawyer but… I never knew what kind of business or what kind of law. I think he might have been an ambulance chaser or maybe he worked for the mob. I went for this type of work because my brother made it sound so heroic and noble and… I think because I did need answers. But I never got those answers from my mother or Jake and I have no idea where my father is."

Penny realized something standing there in the rustic kitchen with Zeke. "It must be so hard on you, tracking your brother and praying you won't be the one to have to bring him down."

Zeke gave her a sideways glance and nodded, his dark eyes misty with emotion. "Yes, I guess I'd like to keep him alive and I've never tried to hide that fact. But… I don't know. Jake wouldn't like prison."

He turned down the burner but went back to mixing and stirring. "I bulldozed my way into this case. But I wanted to be here to help find Jake. We were all concerned about him, of course, and when I told Max about you and Kevin, well, we worried about you two."

Penny leaned against the counter and watched him mixing up the chili. "I need to thank you again…for saving my life the other day and for protecting Kevin and me yet again." She shrugged and a shiver ran through her. "It's only been a few days but it seems as if—"

"As if we've known each other for a long time?"

Their gazes met and held. "Yes. You saved me and you saved my son. I won't ever forget that, Zeke."

He went back to stirring, his expression brooding now. "You mean, after this is over and you go back to your own life? You won't forget me? Or you won't forget what I have to do? I might not be able to save Jake."

Penny took a chance and touched her hand to his arm, the feel of his strong muscles only reminding her of his true character. "I'll never forget *you*, Zeke. Never."

He dropped the spoon onto the spoon holder and turned to her, taking her into his arms. "I sure hope not. Because like I said, I'm tenacious when I want something."

Then he kissed her, his lips on hers, making Penny forget everything but this moment. But the sound of tiny logs crashing to the floor brought them apart and served as a reminder of all that could keep *them* apart.

Zeke's expression held hope and aching tenderness. He kept her close, waiting for her to react, to say something, his gaze washing her in a need that broke her heart.

"Jake was that way, too," she said, her hand cupping Zeke's face. "And that should be enough to remind me of why we can't be together."

Then she turned and hurried to check on her giggling son.

Zeke couldn't sleep. That kiss. He'd felt *her* in that kiss. Had realized she felt the same way he did. She was attracted to him but she didn't want to admit it. So she'd pulled away again, using Jake as her excuse. Maybe out of misguided loyalty or maybe out of pure guilt. No matter. Zeke would bide his time and hope they could find their way through this together.

He couldn't blame her, though, if she didn't

want him in her life. Falling for each other would be a big mistake. First, his career took him away too much—like all the time. How could they have a relationship if he was never around? And…they'd both feel guilty over Jake. Always Jake. Whether his brother lived or died, he'd always have control of both of them.

Unless they could find a way to get past the hurt and betrayal and heartache. None of this was fair or right, but it had to be dealt with before they could have a chance at getting to know each other.

Zeke suddenly gave into his own bitterness and resentment and got up off the couch to stomp around in the dark. Living in Jake's shadow hadn't been easy but he'd pushed through, the way his mother had taught him to do. Unfortunately, he'd hit a wall.

Because now he wanted more than to simply do his job and be a good FBI agent. He wanted more than to impress his tragic, tormented brother who seemed on a path to self-destruction. Now he wanted a life with a wife and son.

Penny and Kevin.

But that was crazy. He'd only met her a few days ago and under the worst possible circumstances. He had to take this slow and get past this current crisis before he could even consider anything more with Penny and Kevin. Right now, he was edgy and exhausted and not thinking very clearly.

He glanced into the open room where mother and child both slept, cuddled together underneath the puffy comforter, Cheetah on the floor at the end of the bed.

What a beautiful sight.

A picture-perfect illusion.

Zeke yanked at the heavy curtains caught up on hooks on each side of the big archway and closed them to give Penny and Kevin some privacy.

She had made it clear she couldn't take things to the next level with him. So why was he pushing this when he had to finish the job and accept the worst-case scenario?

Zeke shifted his thoughts back to the case. He'd gone over and over it with a fine-tooth comb and still didn't have the answers he sought. Where was Jake? Stalking them or long gone?

Opening his phone, he studied the last picture he had of his brother in a candid moment. Jake, wearing a dark T-shirt and smiling. They'd gotten together to watch a football game. Zeke studied the photo, hoping to get a clue. His brother always wore a necklace when he wasn't in uniform. A chain with a silvery snake coiled and hanging from it.

He'd asked Jake about the necklace when he'd first started wearing it.

"A woman once called me Jake the Snake," his brother had said with a steely laugh. "She gave me this right before she walked out on me."

"What kind of man did you become?" he whispered to the grainy image. "Why didn't I take better care of you, see this coming? Try to bring you in before it was too late?"

Putting down the phone with a heavy sigh, Zeke got back to work.

They'd brought down one of Jake's henchmen but another one stood out in his mind.

Gunther Caprice.

Gunther had been a made man within the Dupree family until things started falling apart. He'd been flying under the radar this whole time. Missing and wanted for questioning by the FBI. But he was here in Montana now, right under their noses. Why would he risk his life for Jake?

His former employers had probably tried to track him and kill him, so it made no sense why he was now helping Jake orchestrate this whole thing. Unless... Jake had gotten to him and promised him a ticket out of the country, the same way he'd promised Penny when she'd turned him down.

That nagging gut instinct told him that Jake had to have had some help somewhere. Some high-up intervention, since he kept finding the team and they kept losing him.

Could there be an informant within the unit? Or somewhere within the FBI? Zeke thought back over his conversations with Dylan. Zara had been dealing with something since she'd entered into training at Quantico. All the trouble there had started at about the same time that Jake had gone missing.

But why would Jake try to mess with the trainees at Quantico? Jake and Dylan had been friends. Dylan mentioned that once to Zeke but didn't speak about it since his focus was on helping with the case and keeping track of Zara.

Dylan's fiancée couldn't reveal anything about what was going on but maybe she'd been trying to give them all hints?

He thought back over what little he knew. Dylan had told Leo Gallagher that Zara was afraid she wouldn't graduate on time because something weird was going on with the NATs—new agent trainees. This had started early on and at about the same time Jake had gone missing. He had dates he could document on that, at least.

Zara had cautioned that they didn't need any help. The trainees wanted to handle this on their own. That shouted "Stay out of it."

Maybe this didn't involve all the trainees but only a few? Maybe Zara was in trouble but couldn't tell Dylan that?

Then her roommate had quit unexpectedly. Zeke tapped a note on his phone to remind him to find out more. Maybe the friend would be willing to give him some information. It took a lot for an FBI trainee to quit. They were put through rigorous tests before they were even accepted into the academy. Had someone intimidated or threatened the roommate? Or had the roommate purposely failed as some were inclined to do when they'd had enough? Would she be willing to talk?

Harper reported the trainees had been moved to a safe house. Again, very suspicious. FBI trainees not safe at Quantico? The place was iron tight. What if they'd been moved because the threat seemed to be coming from within?

Last they'd heard, Zara would do her best to be home for her wedding to Dylan. What did that mean? Were the trainees working on a secret case or…were they being protected because they were vulnerable?

Who could get to them like that?

Zeke's gut burned with each unanswered question. His brother could get to just about anybody. Somehow, he had to connect Jake to Zara and the trainees. Penny and the two witnesses at the Wild Iris had identified Gunther Caprice but they needed him to spill the beans.

The rest of this was an out-there premise but Zeke was running out of options. They were like sitting ducks just waiting to be shot down. If something didn't give soon, he'd go to ground and take Penny and Kevin as far away from here as possible.

Meantime, he had to prove that Jake had been messing with Zara to distract the team and gain information from the inside out. He'd have to have solid proof of Jake paying off someone on the inside. Or, if he knew his brother, charming someone on the inside. The roommate? Or someone with a lot more clout and authority?

Exhaling roughly, he shoved a hand through his dark hair. But how could he ever find that proof and try to protect Penny and Kevin, too?

Remembering Max's suggestion, Zeke decided maybe he did need to question Penny about Jake again after all.

FOURTEEN

"You want to do *what*?"

Zeke didn't flinch at Max's growl of a question. Instead, he plunged ahead. "I want to interview Zara's former roommate at Quantico and see if she knows anything about Jake. And I want to find Gunther Caprice. He's on Team Jake now, but if we could get him to agree to a plea bargain, he might spill his guts."

"We're looking for Gunther, Zeke. You know that. I'm not sure about finding the roommate. She left the program. That's pretty clear."

Zeke didn't cave. "But why did she leave? I know there are myriad reasons for an NAT to quit but most don't want it to come to that. Zara implied the woman was running scared."

"You didn't hear that information firsthand," Max reminded him.

"Which is why we need to send someone to interview the woman," Zeke retorted. "Surely the FBI can track down a former trainee."

Max rubbed at his scar. "Look, I get that you want to talk to anyone who can possibly lead you to your brother. The Dupree syndicate has collapsed, but Jake's still out there with one goal left—to get to his son. Why don't you focus on that?"

"I am focusing on that, Max. It's all I think about. Caprice is missing. Zara is in trouble but can't tell us why. The roommate is gone without any explanation. Can you at least agree that someone from Quantico could be helping Jake and that these things could connect us to him?"

Max frowned. "Yes, I'll give you that, but it's still a long shot. We don't have proof but we're pretty sure some of his cronies are still along for the ride. They'd have to be desperate, but they're scattering like rats. Plus we have no idea where Gunther Caprice is right now."

"He's out there somewhere and he sounded extremely frustrated last time I heard him talking on the phone."

Zeke had stumbled on some interesting facts in the reports Dylan had pulled up for him. Caprice had a parting of ways with the Duprees after Reginald was hauled into custody. Maybe because Jake had taken his place within the organization?

But he had found his way back to Jake now that Angus was dead and Reginald was awaiting trial. Gunther could have tracked Jake down and for all Zeke knew, Gunther might have made demands on Jake.

"We need to find him," Zeke continued. "Now that the syndicate has been dismantled, the underlings are getting antsy. If we could just nab one of them and get him—or her—to turn, we might get to the truth. Gunther might have taken off to parts unknown by now. Or he could be hanging around trying to stay on Jake's good side. Or worse."

Zeke knew his theory was far-fetched but he couldn't let go of it now. "We need to ask Violetta about Gunther, too."

Max's expression hardened. "To accomplish what? She was trying to save her sister, Esme, and she did that. She wants nothing else to do with the crimes her uncle and brother committed, and I'm sure she doesn't know a thing about Gunther."

"Remember when I asked you to talk to Violetta?" Zeke said.

Max let out a sigh. "Yes, I called the Dupree estate and requested to speak to Violetta. Apparently she's on a cruise somewhere in the Caribbean." He halted and took a breath. "And, yes, I've got eyes on her."

"That makes sense. She's out of the country, too," Zeke said. "Dylan found strong evidence that she and Gunther were once close but the affair ended badly."

Max didn't even blink. "Yeah, we'd kind of discovered that already but... I don't see how that plays into your theory."

"How can we be sure of anyone from that family?" Zeke asked, his voice rising. "She might be on that cruise ship, waiting for Gunther. Or, worse, my brother."

Max took a look around the cabin, careful to keep his voice low since Penny and Kevin were still asleep. "You're tired and frustrated and grasping at straws. Maybe you're too close to all of this, Zeke."

He lowered his head and put his hands on his hips. "I'm fine but... I have to make sense of this. Jake might be good at putting up distractions, but I'm good at looking at the big picture and putting together pieces of the puzzle that most don't see. I've got Dylan checking into some other things, too. If he doesn't find anything more concrete and if Violetta doesn't cooperate, I'll let this go."

And he'd take Penny and Kevin and leave. For good if he had to. Max looked skeptical but he nodded. "Fair enough." Then he walked to the windows and stared out at the distant foothills and mountains. "How's it going here?"

"We had a quiet night," Zeke said. "Any other leads?"

"No. We've canvassed homes all around the Elk Basin and throughout the wilderness areas around Billings, but every trail runs cold," Max replied, frustration underscoring his words. "I came by to see if you needed to get away for a while. I can keep watch while the crew is switching out. Julianne and Leo will take the next shift."

Zeke checked the closed curtain to the bedroom. Cheetah was working overtime, keeping watch over Penny and Kevin. "Good, sir. Leo and True are strong." Leo Gallagher had been with Jake the day his teammate disappeared and had blamed himself until they'd all realized the truth. "And Julianne has proved herself with Thunder over and over." He smiled. "That foxhound is one smart animal and Julianne Martinez is a great agent."

"I'm glad you approve," Max said on a dry note. "Still, you might want to get out of here for a while."

"No, sir," Zeke replied, deliberately not taking the hint. "I'll keep busy working on this angle while I wait to hear from Dylan regarding Quantico."

"All right," Max said. "But next time, that won't be a suggestion."

Zeke got that the SAC wanted him in control and not so on edge but…his instincts had never let him down before. When he thought back, he'd sensed something going on with Jake but chalked his moods up to him becoming a dad. Jake had never talked about wanting children but Kevin had changed his notion on that. But a good father wouldn't force his child away from his mother. Or try to kill the woman who'd given him a son.

Zeke wouldn't stop until he found his brother. Dead or alive. His phone buzzed. Dylan.

"I've just heard from Violetta Dupree," Dylan said on a winded voice. "She texted me a clue."

"What?"

Lights and siren syndrome. That's what Jake the Snake is all about.

Zeke's whole body went cold. His gut burned hot. That was a term sometimes used in FBI training. It referred to how some people never got over the adrenaline rush of becoming an agent. Jake had always been one of those people. The hint screamed Quantico.

And proved that Zeke was on the right track.

* * *

"What's going on?"

Penny stood at the bedroom door staring over at Zeke. He was turned, speaking low into his phone. She'd heard voices earlier and after checking on Kevin, she'd opened the privacy curtains to the den. That's when she'd overheard Zeke and Max talking about Quantico. She'd remembered that one memory she'd either blocked or maybe held back out of embarrassment and regret. But now, after hearing more rumblings she thought Zeke should know. If he'd level with her in return.

Zeke put away his phone and turned and faced her but she saw the tension in his expression. "Max was here. We're trying to establish some things that might help us to find Jake. I need to ask you—"

Penny's heart hammered against her ribs. "But we still don't know where Jake is, right?"

Zeke gave her a puzzled stare. "No. I've got people working on some new angles."

"I'm only asking because I heard you mention Quantico again," she said. "I remembered something else, something I should have told you about sooner."

Zeke's eyes went wide. "I was just about to

ask if you knew about certain things. Talk to me, Penny."

Seeing the eagerness mixed with a tinge of disappointment in his eyes, she hoped she hadn't waited too late on this. "Once when Jake was at my house, I was washing clothes and I picked up a pair of his jeans. A photo of Jake and a woman fell out. I immediately expected the worst—that he was cheating on me. When I asked him about the picture, he got angry and told me to leave his clothes alone. Then later, he apologized and explained that he had fallen for another trainee years before. But things ended badly and they both went their separate ways. I accepted that and let it go but... he'd obviously kept that photo a long time."

Zeke's expression hardened and his eyes held a trace of dread. "Did he tell you her name or anything else?"

Penny shook her head. "No. He refused to talk about it." She tugged her hair behind her ear. "It happened right after Kevin was born and honestly, I didn't think much about it after that since Jake seemed so devoted to our son. But now I wonder about it. That day when he called and sounded so upset and off-kilter, he did mention Quantico and how he believed he still had friends there. Do you think he kept in touch with this woman?"

Zeke's features softened but he pressed her. "You said he'd lost trust in someone, too."

"Yes." Penny hated to admit it. "I wonder if he wasn't having an affair with this woman all along and when I got pregnant, he ended it. Or maybe she did." Her heart bumping a warning, she asked, "Do you think he could have reached out to his friend again? She'd be long gone by now, but he could have contacted her recently, given his situation."

Zeke pulled out his phone and started tapping away as if he didn't even know she was in the room. "I'll get Dylan on it but…you just might have helped us get to the bottom of this case, Penny."

"I should have told you sooner," she said, her voice tinged with regret. "But… I kind of blocked any thoughts of him with other women."

"It's okay," he said. "I planned to jar your memory anyway so we were on the same page. This is a major breakthrough."

"Zeke, tell me what's going on."

"I can't," he said, putting his phone away. "Too many details. But…we're so close."

"Close to finding Jake or close to building a solid case against him?"

"The case is solid enough but yes, we need to keep everything by the book."

Penny sensed a distinct difference in him even while his eyes filled with excitement. Maybe he couldn't talk about the details. He'd been careful with what he shared with her but…she heard things, suspected things. She'd opened up with this information, hoping he'd do the same with her.

Not sure what to say, she headed straight to the coffeepot.

He moved closer. "How'd you sleep?"

"Okay." But in actuality, she'd tossed and turned all night, aware of their kiss in the kitchen last night. Aware of her wants and needs and the myriad reasons why she couldn't fall for Zeke.

And he obviously wasn't in a talking mood this morning. Probably regretting that kiss.

They'd eaten the chili with very little conversation and Zeke hadn't kissed her again. Kevin had taken up much of their time and energy before he'd worn himself out. Penny had put him to bed and after a few quiet moments together where Zeke tapped on his phone, she'd gone into the bedroom to read a book.

Now she wished she could take back what she'd said after they'd kissed, but she'd spoken the truth. She could wish she'd never kissed Zeke, but…that wonderful, warm memory wouldn't leave her mind. That kiss had scared her way too much. And made her feel alive again even when her heart was so caught up in misery and regret.

Jake had been tenacious, too. She'd panicked and pulled away from Zeke because she was so afraid of going through that kind of pain again. But she shouldn't have said those spiteful words to Zeke.

Jake's impulses were quick and swift and he made decisions based on those impulses. But Zeke was determined and thorough and he made decisions based on facts and logic. One went after what he wanted out of life, regardless of who he hurt, and the other one went after those who committed crimes and ruined lives and tried to be kind and considerate in spite of the dangers. A bad trait in Jake. A good trait in Zeke. She heaved a frustrated sigh. Why did she have to always compare them anyway?

But what if Zeke up and changed one day, the way Jake had? Jake managed to hide his issues but the day she told him she was pregnant, Penny saw his true nature.

Now she had to consider what she'd pushed out of her mind so long ago. Had he resented her pregnancy because he was still in love with another woman?

"He never wanted a child," she blurted, hoping to see Zeke in a different light. She knew the truth but her heart was so broken and battered she didn't want to acknowledge the truth. She needed to test him a little more. "He got really upset when I told him I was pregnant."

Zeke turned to face her. "I know. He told me about it."

Humiliated, she recoiled, a hand to her mouth. So Zeke pitied her? "You've known that all along?"

"Yes, but—"

"But you didn't tell me." She didn't know why that hurt so much. She needed to remember that her feelings for Zeke couldn't see her through. This new revelation was just one more reason she had to find her own way in life. She shared a painful, uncertain memory with Zeke and now this. Embarrassed and tired, she turned away.

But a strong hand pulled her around. "Penny, how can I convince you that I'm not like him? When he told me, I worried about you and the baby and prayed that he'd do the right thing. But it wasn't my place back then to interfere. Jake said he had things under control." He shrugged. "I should have told you but… I didn't want to add to your agony over this."

"So all this time, you're helping me out of pity and duty?"

"Duty, yes. Pity, no," he said, a firm determination in his words. "You're so wrapped up in Jake and what he's done to you that you can't see me. The *real* me. I'd like to stay a part of your life when this is over. For Kevin's sake and…because I care about you, Penny."

When she didn't respond, he tugged her close. "I could have told you a lot right up front, but I was more focused on keeping you alive. I can't give you all the details." Then he brought it home. "And I could say the same for you. This intel about another woman is huge. Yet you kept it from me until you heard me discussing Quantico with Max."

"I'm sorry," she said, some of her anger dissipating. "It was painful and I… I tried to put it out of my mind. I played blind but now I can see it all so clearly. You're right. I can't seem to get past the man who betrayed me and is now trying to kill me. I'm not in a good place to make decisions right now."

Stepping back, Zeke nodded. "Okay, neither am I. But don't take anything I do or say as pity. I admire you."

She smiled at that. "Thank you."

"Jake tried," Zeke replied. "You said he gave you money to help take care of Kevin."

Bobbing her head, she quit smiling and pivoted to stare out at the mountains. "Yes, he did. Guilt money. Dirty money."

Zeke stood behind her. "Yes. But perhaps that was his way of showing you that he wasn't all bad."

"Now you're making excuses for him?"

"I'm trying to understand him. I'm not proud of what he's become but… I'd like to think he still has some trace of decency in him."

"Well, you're wrong. I think the good in him has been long dead."

She didn't want to break down but her emotions were bubbling like a running brook. She'd held it together, piece by piece, for months now. This kind of intimate talk could only lead to her falling into Zeke's arms.

"You were there in the chalet in Colorado, weren't you?"

Shocked, she came around so Zeke could see her face-to-face. He seemed to want to pick a fight with her but she wasn't going to fall for it.

"I was, but I took Kevin and left when I thought Jake had found us."

"Why did you think he was coming there?"

Feeling cornered, she glared at him. "Why do you care?"

"I need to know. I told you I'd want to know more."

"I got a call on my cell. But no one was there. The connection ended and I panicked."

"So you thought it was Jake?"

"Of course, I thought it was Jake. It wasn't as if I was waiting for him. More, like, expecting him to track me down. Which he has, time after time, or we wouldn't be standing here."

Zeke's expression changed, shifted, relaxed.

He must have been going over every detail of this case and while he'd been doing that, he'd also tried to figure out a few things about her, obviously.

"How'd you get away?" he finally asked.

Penny wanted to end this conversation but she had to be truthful. "I'm a wilderness guide, remember? We found a path down the mountain into town." Getting closer so he'd fully understand how terrifying her ordeal had been that day, she added, "I carried my son in my arms for three miles, Zeke. Three miles of mountains and rough terrain, streams and jagged rocks and several near encounters with wild animals."

He almost said something but instead he asked, "And you paid the hotel clerk to lie about you booking a room?"

"Yes, to throw Jake off my trail. I'm not proud of lying but… I didn't know what else to do. Why are you asking me about all this now?"

"I told you I'd planned to interrogate you again."

"Yes, you did." She tried to turn away, but

he put a hand on each of her arms, the strength in his touch warming her in spite of this roiling tension between them.

"I need you to understand something, Penny. We're closing in on Jake and before we do, I need to know how you really feel about him."

"For the case?" she asked, thinking he was as ruthless as Jake. "To prove that I've done something wrong…or to show that I'm telling the truth?"

"No." He leaned in, his face inches from hers, his dark eyes burning hot. Then he put his hand on her face and held her there, the brush of his fingers like a promise. "For *me*. I need to know for my own sanity. Because I want to believe you don't still have feelings for him. I need to believe that. I need to know that…before *I* give into these feelings *I* have for you."

Penny didn't know what to say. She'd often asked herself that same question, regarding Jake and…regarding Zeke. What did she feel? She wanted to tell him she had strong feelings for him, too. Feelings that were different from the fast and furious attraction she'd thought she'd had for Jake. That crush of strong emotions was gone now, to be replaced by something slow and simmering and equally strong. Zeke had won her over the moment he'd called out her name in the wilderness. But she wasn't ready to admit that right now.

She didn't love Jake. Not anymore. Maybe she never had. She'd loved the idea of being in love and having a handsome, dynamic man take notice of her. But now that Zeke had spoken these things out loud, she had to swallow hard and bite down on her emotions. How could she be sure that this wasn't the same kind of infatuation and that she'd regret running right into Zeke's arms? She wanted to say the right thing, but fear gripped her, rendering her speechless.

But Zeke took her silence for something else.

"I see," he said. Then he turned around and stalked away.

Bitter and hurting, Penny couldn't let it go that easily. "And what about you, Zeke? You watched him get away the other day when you could have shot him. Why don't you analyze your own feelings instead of nitpicking mine?"

He didn't even turn around. "I've analyzed everything about my life since the day I found out I had a brother, and right now I'm trying to reconcile that I might have to be the one to bring him down."

Penny's heart skipped a beat. She almost ran to him to comfort him. But Kevin cried out, giving her a reprieve from having to watch Zeke walk away.

FIFTEEN

Zeke's cell buzzed later that day, a welcome distraction from Penny's stormy silence. She didn't want to care about him, and maybe she was right to keep pushing him away. He'd been telling himself the same thing, hadn't he? So he put the memory of their kiss and their last heated conversation out of his mind and answered his phone. He'd immediately consulted with Max about the cryptic hint Violetta had shared with Dylan. Finally, things were moving along.

"Dylan, do you have something?"

"Yes," he said. "I pulled in a lot of favors and kept Zara out of this so she wouldn't get any heat, but we've located her roommate. Her name is Brandy Ridgeway. She's been hiding out in Colorado."

Zeke did a sweep of the room. Penny was taking a shower and Julianne was entertaining Kevin, her K-9 partner, Thunder, guarding them. "Hiding out? Why?"

"The woman fears for her life," Dylan said. "We sent two local agents to talk to her and she tried to run. After they explained that they were there just to question her, she finally told them why she'd left Quantico."

Zeke held his breath, wondering if his brother had pulled some strings. "And?"

"It took some doing, but Brandy finally admitted that one of the instructors has been keeping in touch with Jake Morrow."

Zeke rubbed his forehead, his gut clenching. "That's not surprising. What else? Who is the instructor?"

"A woman named Rebecca Carwell who trained with Jake years ago. They were close. For a long, long time. So the information Penny gave you about the Quantico thing is correct." Dylan lowered his voice. "Here's the thing. Zara and Brandy stumbled on some information that suggested this instructor and Jake had been communicating in recent months. Maybe even meeting in out-of-the-way places."

Zeke closed his eyes. Had his brother been two-timing Penny the whole time? She'd suspected that but hearing it out loud infuriated Zeke. Not to mention an FBI instructor not alerting them about Jake. The woman had to know from the beginning that he'd gone missing. And later, that he was wanted and considered armed and dangerous. "Go on. Give me all of it."

"Special Agent Rebecca Carwell doesn't have any stains on her record. She worked in a California field office for a while and still has ties there. She's been back as an instructor for three years now. But she did graduate with Jake, and...others who knew them said they had been an item for a while."

So that matched what Jake had told Penny about not trusting anyone—no, *someone*—at Quantico anymore. Someone he'd depended on. Fraternizing amongst trainees was a big no-no, but it happened and sometimes those ties were hard to break.

This made perfect sense when he matched it to Violetta's clue. Jake still had someone on the inside at Quantico.

"Explain what happened," Zeke said, already getting the picture.

Dylan went on. "Apparently this all started when the word got out that Jake had been taken by Angus Dupree. Special Agent Carwell got all antsy and upset. Zara and Brandy heard her talking on her phone one night and...they started putting things together. It started as a joke. Rebecca tended to be very strict and by the book, so they wondered if she ever had any fun. Once the NATs were able to take leave on the weekends, those two followed her just for something to do. But when they saw who she was snuggling up with in a dark park, they panicked."

Zeke's anger flared but he stayed quiet, allowing the other man to go on.

"The man could have been Jake Morrow but they weren't sure," Dylan explained. "So they decided they'd watch and wait for verification since Jake was still considered missing. Zara couldn't say a word to us since she couldn't be sure the man was Jake." He took a long breath. "Plus, she found it hard to believe Jake would be anywhere near Quantico."

"Does this roommate think that was the case?" Zeke asked, wishing his hunch hadn't paid off. "That Jake and Rebecca were in cahoots even after the FBI realized he'd flipped?"

"Yes," Dylan replied. "But we have to gather more intel, Zeke. So don't do anything yet, okay? The recruits are still in a safe house."

"I won't," Zeke said, trying to remember the agent in question. He'd never heard Jake mention her but then, why would he? "Is Max aware of this?"

"Yes. I went straight to him…since he'd ordered me to do that before I brought any of this to you. But before anyone does anything, Zara needs to graduate and get home. Somehow the NATs got involved in this secret sideline investigation and things went downhill from there. They'd have to report this, unless, of course, they don't trust anyone." Dylan stopped and took a breath. "I just want Zara back here and safe in time for our wedding."

Zeke understood the need to be discreet. Dylan had been waiting on Zara to return for months now. She could be in danger, especially if someone found out their unit had recently talked to her roommate. "So…what? We're watching and waiting?"

"Yes. Max has informed people, and he arranged to personally fly to Quantico last night and interrogate Agent Carwell in private. He should arrive back at headquarters here any time now. Meantime, we have Brandy Ridgeway's statement and Max has sent someone to protect her. She's willing to testify since her career is ruined."

"So this caused her to leave? Was she threatened while still at Quantico?"

Dylan let out a grunt. "Rebecca approached Brandy after Brandy and Zara started putting things together. She turned the tables, saying she'd heard rumors that *they* might know of Jake's whereabouts due to Zara's connection to our team. Rebecca hinted that Brandy should keep tabs on Zara in case we passed her any information. In case I slipped up and divulged anything classified, which of course I didn't."

He blew out a huff of frustration and cleared his throat. "But Agent Carwell didn't know that they'd already figured things out. Brandy took the fall since she wasn't sure she wanted to stay in the program anyway. She never squealed on Zara because Zara hadn't done anything wrong. She told Carwell she didn't come to the academy to turn on another agent. She agreed to forget the whole thing if Rebecca would let her leave, but Rebecca wouldn't agree to that. She began making things difficult for Zara and Brandy."

"Such as?" Zeke asked.

Dylan dived right in, explaining. "Their dorm room being searched. Both being used as an example during training runs, being harassed when a scenario case wasn't solved immediately. Accused of trying to give confidential information to someone on the outside. Which they didn't do. They proved they didn't do anything but she didn't let up."

"So Carwell wouldn't let Brandy leave? Did she try to blackmail her or something?"

"She made life hard and threatened both of them with exposure, yes," Dylan replied. "At least according to Brandy. I hope Zara can tell us everything once she gets to come home."

"But Brandy did drop out," Zeke said. "How did that come about?"

"The old-fashioned way," Zeke said. "Brandy failed some of the training courses and got herself kicked out. Carwell couldn't stop her without exposing what they knew about *her*, too. But after that, again according to Brandy, Zara worked hard to stay in the program. I don't know why they're in lockdown."

"What was Jake hoping to gain?" Zeke asked, his head throbbing.

"Who knows. A distraction. Information on where we were and if we were tracking him. He used Agent Carwell and he tried to trip up Zara and Brandy, too. But Zara stuck to the plan and didn't spill anything because she didn't know anything. She could only prove that she wasn't passing information." He exhaled heavily. "I can't believe she's been dealing with this all along, but that's what she's training for. So we have to keep quiet and solve the case."

Zeke didn't like it, but he agreed. They couldn't march in on the word of an ex-trainee and snatch a senior instructor who'd been a loyal agent for over a decade. They needed Zara's take on this, but he doubted even Max could have nabbed an interview with her. Too risky. If Max had gotten to Rebecca Carwell, it would be in a secretive meeting to hear her side, not accuse her. Even that could get Zara in hot water, but her former roommate *had* volunteered the information.

He thanked Dylan and told him he'd check with Max. "And, Dylan, send me a picture of Carwell and the roommate, any pictures the agents who interrogated Ridgeway might have taken for evidence, too."

"Sure. I guess Violetta did us another favor, grudgingly, of course."

Zeke shook his head. "Yes. It would have been nice to hear this earlier, but we can only assume that she's been in touch with Caprice and he let something slip. Probably how she kept tabs on all of them."

"Yep, but I guess she's not willing to forgive and forget. According to our sources in Chicago who've been watching her closely, Violetta refuses to even let Caprice in the gate. She left on that cruise to get away from all of this. But…she obviously hasn't let it all go."

"Thanks again," Zeke said. "This information means we're getting somewhere at least."

When he turned back to the room, Julianne stood and walked over to him, her dark eyes full of questions. "Some news?"

"Yes. But not the good kind." Glancing toward the curtained bedroom, he added, "And I can't go into detail right now."

Julianne nodded and touched a hand to her dark, upswept hair. "Understood."

Zeke gave her a thankful nod and went to play with Kevin. Though Penny already suspected this, he planned to hold off on telling her that Jake had possibly been involved with another agent while with Penny. She obviously still cared about Jake from the way she'd gone silent on him earlier then turned the tables on his own feelings regarding his brother. A part of her still loved Jake and maybe she needed to hang on to that feeling a little bit longer. Until this was all over and she could see things clearly again.

Once that happened, he'd tell her the truth. That Jake had used all of them and he was no good for any of them. Especially no good for her and Kevin. It was a bitter truth, but just like Penny, Zeke had been in denial about his brother. This latest news ended all doubts on trying to save Jake. Prison or worse, Zeke had to do what needed to be done to bring down his brother.

But he also had to continue safeguarding Penny, even going so far as to protect her love for Jake. For her and Kevin's sake.

He couldn't add to her doubts and trauma by telling her this and verifying her worst pain. She'd had enough heartbreak without hearing about this new wrinkle.

Besides, it was highly classified information. Period. He'd go with that rationale for now and ignore how his own emotions were beginning to take over his usual logic.

Penny spent most of the day getting to know Zeke's team member, Julianne Martinez, and enjoying Kevin while she tried to ignore the way Zeke was avoiding her. While Julianne was a delight and had caught her up on all the newly formed relationships developing within the team, including her own reunion with former love Brody Kenner, Penny wished Zeke would talk to her. They hadn't had any time alone so she wasn't able to explain her true feelings to him. But now wasn't the time to convince him she no longer loved Jake. And now sure wasn't the time to tell him she had strong feelings for him but she was afraid to act on those feelings.

So after Julianne went outside to do a sweep, she kept to herself and hugged on Kevin, showering her confused son with love. At least this forced isolation had given her some precious quality time with him. He was growing so fast, even the few clothes she'd brought with them were going to get snug soon. Would she ever be able to go back to the Wild Iris and get what few belongings they had left?

Dusk was settling over the mountains now and she had yet to talk to Zeke. He'd been scrolling on his laptop and verifying things on his phone all day, and now he'd disappeared into the bathroom. Penny wished she could go outside and take in the fresh mountain air, especially since this time of year the temperature would start going down with the changing seasons. August temperatures sometimes changed dramatically from day to day. Fall was wonderful in Montana. Unless you were in hiding from a desperate man.

"How you holding up?" Zeke asked, surprising her as he came out of the bathroom, all fresh and clean from his shower. They'd only shared clipped small talk for most of the day so his question threw her. But the way he looked threw her even more.

The man was gorgeous.

"I'm okay," she said, trying to keep her tone neutral.

Penny breathed in the crisp scent of spicy soap and decided that would have to do as far as getting some fresh air. His dark, close-cropped waves, still damp from the shower, caressed his ears and forehead in a way she wished she could. He wore a clean black T-shirt and faded jeans. But the gun in his shoulder holster only reminded her of why they were here.

He didn't remind her of Jake, however. In fact, she wasn't thinking of her ex at all in this moment with Zeke's mysterious eyes capturing hers with a hint of remorse and regret.

He held something back, something he wasn't ready to tell her.

Swallowing back the implications of that realization, she stood and smiled at him. She could be civil at least. "I'm good, all things considered. Kevin is safe and you've all been very considerate to me."

Zeke moved toward her, his gaze never leaving her face. "Considerate? Is that what you think this is between us? Just a consideration for a woman who's being threatened?"

"You know what I mean," she replied, hoping he wasn't about to accuse her again and hoping she could apologize for her earlier remarks. "Your team has been watching out for me for almost a week now. *You've* gone beyond being considerate, Zeke."

But he had become distant since their last conversation. He'd been on edge all day, in a mood she couldn't quite read. That, and not knowing what he might have found, scared her but she'd done some heavy praying for the Lord to help her see him in a different light. In a light outside the shadow of his big brother.

Zeke was his own man. A good man. Why couldn't she just go with that and put her trust in him? And God.

Zeke hooked his thumbs into his jeans pockets and looked down at the floor. "Yeah, well, you've gone beyond letting me know that I'm looking at a lost cause. You're still in love with Jake. End of conversation. So I'm going to do my job and leave the rest to fate."

She shook her head and lowered her voice. "For someone who's so smart, you sure are being thickheaded about my feelings."

"You shouted your feelings loud and clear when I asked you directly, Penny," he said in a snarl of a whisper. "You couldn't even look me in the eye and tell me the truth."

She had to tell him the truth now, though. "Zeke—"

"I have to get back to work," he said, interrupting her. "Dylan just sent me some photos." He sat down at the big table and opened his laptop.

Angry, Penny came to stand behind him, her gaze hitting on the pictures. A close-up of a pretty woman and more photos of the same woman. Then she spotted something that caused her to take in a breath. "Zeke?"

He shook his head and tried to shut the laptop. "I don't have time to talk about this right now, Penny."

"Zeke," she said again, her hand on his so he couldn't close down the open file. "I recognize that necklace."

Penny pointed to the intricate necklace around the woman's neck. "The silver snake," she said in a shocked whisper. "Jake the Snake. That belonged to him."

"What?" Zeke leaned in and let out a held breath. "It does look like the one he wore. Are you sure?"

"Yes," she said, bobbing her head, her stomach clenching with the final gut-wrenching truth. "He always wore it. Who is she?"

Zeke's phone buzzed before he could respond.

"What?" he rasped into the phone, his gaze holding Penny's while his tone and expression showed a heavy frustration. He listened, silent and stern, his gaze moving over Penny, his frown turning dark with concern. "Yes, I understand." After a few more minutes of intense back and forth, he asked, "How much time do we have?"

Penny knew what was coming. She could

tell from his actions that something significant had happened. He started stalking around the room while he barked replies to whoever was on the line. He finally ended the call and turned toward her. "We've got trouble."

Julianne hurried through the door, apprehension clear in her eyes. "I got a call on the radio. Six of them, Zeke, armed to the teeth. They're surrounding us."

An explosion down below rocked the air.

Penny's heart stopped. Were they going to bomb the cabin? She rushed to grab Kevin so fast that she startled him. "Mommy!" he cried out, fretting as his eyes widened.

Cheetah and Thunder both stood at alert. Penny pivoted to Zeke. "Zeke, I—"

He lifted a hand to her face then dropped it, his eyes full of regret.

Then she heard a round of shots being fired down below the deck. "He's found us again."

"Yes." Zeke grabbed her close, his jaw clenched tight. For a moment, she thought he'd tell her everything, whatever he'd just heard but instead, he stood there for a lifetime of precious seconds, his true feelings shining through the darkness in his eyes.

Then he said, "This is all going to be over soon."

Penny had tried to put this nightmare out of

her mind, but in her heart she'd known it was coming. And this time, she had a feeling Jake wouldn't send others. This time, he'd be the one to storm her sanctuary and take her child right out of her arms.

SIXTEEN

Zeke took in the scene, his mind still reeling with what Max had rapidly reported. Rebecca Carwell wasn't in cahoots with Jake. She'd met Jake in the park that night and tried to get him to turn himself in. When he refused and held a gun on her, she let him go and wished too late that she'd brought backup. Max had interrogated her in a secret location and she'd told him the truth—that she had to keep this a secret or end her career. She begged Max to stop messing in something she needed to finish.

But Max couldn't stop what had been set into motion.

Zeke had to move, the fast-paced conversation he'd had with Max still looping through his head. He'd get the details later. Right now, he had to get Penny and Kevin out of this cabin.

If they were surrounded and the team members hiding in the woods couldn't get to them, they had no way out. The shots fired could mean the team had taken down some of the people coming for them.

Or it could mean the two extra guards they'd had stationed at the main door were gone.

He went with the worst-case scenario and called out to Julianne. "We have to go. Now!"

"I'll check the mudroom entrance," Julianne told him, already headed that way. "They must have cut the security system."

"Yeah," Zeke said. "Not good."

Zeke drew his gun and shoved Penny, who was holding a frightened Kevin, behind him. Then he commanded Cheetah forward to guard. "Stay with me," he ordered. "No matter what, Penny. Stay with me."

That plea echoed inside his head as he heard more shots, these near the front door of the cabin. Cheetah glanced back but the dog stayed silent and moved forward, following Julianne and Thunder.

Getting between Penny and whoever came through the door, Zeke pushed her to the side door. "Remember how we discussed this," he said. "We go down to the basement and exit out the back through the heavy vines hiding the door. The path is hidden there. If something happens, you take the path down. Keep going and don't look back."

She nodded and held her now-crying son close to her chest. "Got it. Zeke—"

"Shhh," he said as they rounded the corner to the small mudroom past the wide pantry.

"Hurry," Julianne whispered. "Both guards are down. We don't have much time."

The front door up on the other side of the house burst open just as they rushed through the hidden side door beyond the pantry. Zeke heard footsteps panning out. More than one set.

Off in the distance, more shots rang out and dogs barked. They made it through the door and onto a small landing. Julianne shut the door behind them and shoved an old wrought iron deck chair against it to give them precious seconds.

Zeke pushed Penny and Kevin ahead of him down the enclosed spiral stairs. They made it to the bottom and he shielded them against a wall while Julianne and Thunder hurried around him and opened the door leading into the woods. Julianne gripped her rifle and shifted left to right.

"Clear," she said in a harsh whisper. Thunder stood with her. She turned to Zeke after he pulled Penny and Kevin close behind him. Then she shut the door to the cabin. "I leave you here. I'll hide behind those rocks over there and fire a round or two to give you cover. Thunder and I can double back and find the rest of the team."

Zeke wanted to tell Julianne no, but this was her job and she'd only resent him if he did that. "Okay. As long as you have backup on the way."

"Roger that," she said, already heading for cover.

Zeke looked down at Penny, Kevin between them. "Hold on to your son and stay as close to me as possible."

Penny bobbed her head, her eyes holding his. "Zeke?"

He kissed her, hard and fast. "I'm going to get you out of here."

They worked their way down the rutted, rocky path leading to a small waterfall and stream. Zeke radioed for a vehicle to be waiting for them on a dirt road at the bottom of the ravine. He prayed they'd make it that far without being ambushed.

Cheetah led the way, his snout up and sniffing for any danger. Zeke kept Penny in front of him and she shielded Kevin in her arms. They'd left without any provisions except Kevin's blanket and the night air was chilly, but she moved through the moonlight without a word, her hand on her son's head in a protective measure that broke Zeke's heart.

I promise, Lord. If I get them out of here alive, I will spend the rest of my days trying to show them the love they deserve.

Kevin's sobs had turned into feeble whimpers and now, with the constant bump against rocks and jutted earth, the kid seemed to be drifting off to sleep against his mother's shoulder. Zeke longed to take the boy, to lift that sweet weight off her shoulders and put the precious burden on his own. But he needed to stay free in case he had to use his weapon.

He'd have to be the one to stay and fight while they got away.

They silently worked their way down the path, the moonlight both a blessing and a curse. They'd rounded a bend when gunfire erupted off in the woods.

Zeke grabbed Penny's arm. "Get down," he hissed. Then to Cheetah, "Stay. Guard."

Cheetah stood in front of Penny and Kevin while Zeke searched ahead, trying to watch for shadows or movement in the scrub brush and bramble along the way.

"Nothing up ahead," he said, relief washing over him. "We're almost to the cutoff road. Someone should be waiting there to get you to safety."

"What about you and your team members?" Penny asked. "Julianne and…the rest. Zeke, I can't bear it if one of them gets shot. I can't let you—"

"They're pros," he said, trying to keep his tone confident. "They know what to do. And you don't need to worry about me, either."

"But that explosion—and we keep hearing gunfire."

"Part of the process," he said, wondering if anyone would survive this. When his radio crackled to life, Zeke immediately reported in.

"Agent Morrow." It was Max West. "Are you safe?"

"Ten-four, sir. Package is secure." Then he asked, "Everyone accounted for?"

"Affirmative. Two guards down. Team secure," Max replied. He didn't linger. "Report in when extraction is complete."

"Yes, sir."

Zeke turned to Penny. "See, they're all okay. And we'll be on our way out of here soon."

"And where will we go next, Zeke?" she asked, her voice quiet and husky. "Where can I hide?"

"I don't know," he admitted. "But I will promise you this. I'm going to take you and Kevin as far away from here as possible."

The look in her eyes told him what he

needed to know. She wanted that, too. But he also saw the despair in her gaze. Zeke leaned over to kiss her but froze in place. The breaking of a twig crunched a few yards off the path. Cheetah's ears went up and the dog emitted a low growl.

Penny heard it, too. She inhaled a breath and held tight to Kevin. Zeke crouched and turned only to see a dark figure rushing toward him. The butt of a rifle came down on Zeke's temple, hard and swift, causing him to fall forward, his weapon sliding out of his grip. Jake. Cheetah's barks turned aggressive. Zeke caught a glimpse of a dark figure behind Jake and heard a swish of sound. Cheetah fell to the ground before Zeke could order him to attack. Zeke blinked and tried to call out, but Cheetah lifted his head then fell back, a dark stain covering a white spot on his back.

Zeke looked up at his brother standing over him, seeing a dark rage in Jake's eyes, the sound of Penny's screams radiating through the searing pain in his brain. He tried to stand but couldn't find the strength to push himself up.

Jake kicked him back down and stalked toward Penny. Throwing his rifle strap over his shoulder, he lowered the gun and said, "It's time to get this over with, once and for all."

"No!" Penny started falling backward and tripped. Kevin slipped out of her arms to the ground.

The boy plopped on his bottom and cried out. "Mommy!" His sobs echoed down the hill and tore straight through Zeke's heart.

Zeke watched in horror, dizziness pushing at his consciousness, as he saw Jake reach down and grab Penny.

"Get my son," Jake called to the man with him. Then he turned back to Penny and grabbed her around her throat. "This will be the last time you try to hide my boy from me."

Zeke grunted and lifted up, blinking back the throbbing pain that surrounded his brain. Jake's hands circled Penny's neck, trying to strangle her. Zeke saw the terror in her eyes, saw her trying to claw her way to Kevin. Penny's hand caught on a rock and she tried to reach out and hit Jake with it, but he shoved her hand away and the rock fell to the earth.

Zeke called out. "Stop, Jake. Please, stop." He searched for his weapon and noticed Cheetah trying to get up. "C'mon on, boy," Zeke said. "Come. Attack."

He had to do something. He'd failed all of them and now he'd be forced to watch Penny die right in front of his eyes. Jake would win after all.

"I said, 'Grab Kevin,'" Jake called to the man standing there with a gun in his hand. He wore a dark cap and dark heavy clothing.

Zeke lifted to his knees and spotted his weapon. Then he saw the man's face. Gunther Caprice! He'd shoot to kill.

"Stop," Zeke called. "Jake, don't do this."

Jake ignored Zeke, his hands still on Penny. "Caprice, get Kevin and take him down the mountain. You know the plan."

Gunther started toward Kevin. "I'll get him all right. But I'm taking him with *me* and none of you will see him again until I get the money you promised me months ago, Morrow. I'm tired of this."

Penny started thrashing against Jake, her eyes wide with terror, her hands over Jake's. But she'd never be able to fight him off.

"I mean it, Jake," Gunther Caprice called out. "You're holding out on me. I know it. I want my money now so I can get out of this place. I hate it here." He lifted his weapon to where Kevin now stood, crying and calling out for Penny. "Your mama's kind of caught up in something, little fellow."

He held the gun down toward Kevin.

Zeke grunted with all his might, stretching to reach his weapon. Jake turned to Gunther and watched as Gunther went for Kevin, his gun aimed at the boy.

"If you don't give me my money, I'll kill the kid," Gunther shouted while he stomped toward Kevin.

Zeke slid toward his weapon. Jake screamed a curse and let go of Penny, violently pushing her to the ground. Then he whipped his rifle back around and held it toward the other man.

"Don't you go near my son, Gunther," Jake shouted, his hands trembling. "He's the only good thing I have left and I won't let you hurt him."

"Too late," Gunther said. "I want you to suffer the same way I've had to suffer. You ruined everything, Morrow. Everything." Inching closer to Kevin, he said, "Drop your weapon, right now."

Jake lifted his gun away and dropped it to the ground, but Gunther kept his weapon trained on Kevin. The click of Gunther's silenced handgun echoed out over the night like a death knell.

Everything after that happened in a rapid-fire cadence that left Zeke dazed and in a state of shock. He called out to Cheetah and heard Cheetah's growls behind him. Jake watched Gunther, shadows coloring his haggard face, then dived toward Kevin just as Gunther pulled the trigger.

A gunshot rang out in the night.

Jake went down a couple of feet away from Kevin, his eyes on his crying son. He reached out a hand then let it fall. Then he went still.

Stunned, Gunther stared down at Jake and lifted his weapon toward Kevin again.

Penny screamed and crawled toward her son. Then she grabbed the powerful rifle Jake had dropped and turned it toward Gunther Caprice. She shot him once, twice, tears streaming down her face. Gunther fell down onto his knees. Penny dropped the gun and ran for Kevin.

But Gunther grunted and tried to get back up, his face twisted in pain and rage, his right shoulder gushing blood.

"Attack," Zeke managed to call out, praying Cheetah had the strength. The dog started barking and rushed the man and brought him down, his big teeth sinking into Gunther's flailing left arm.

Zeke checked on Penny and Kevin, his eyes meeting hers in relief, then he rushed to Jake.

She lifted up her crying son to hold him close. "It's okay. Mommy's here. You're safe now."

Zeke grabbed his phone, his hands trembling. Then he dropped it by his side and lifted Jake's head. He could hear sirens squealing down on the road. "Don't die on me now," he said, tears in his eyes. "Jake, you hear me?"

"I hear you, bro," Jake said in a weak whisper. "Kevin?"

"He's safe. You saved his life."

Jake grinned. "Got some good left in me, huh?"

"Yes." Zeke glanced up at Penny, his heart hurting for her and his brother. "Yeah, you did one last good deed. Your son will be proud of you."

Jake grabbed Zeke's shirt. "Need to tell you where the rest of them are. Record this."

Zeke turned on his phone recorder. "I'm listening."

In a weak whisper, Jake gave Zeke the locations of several warehouses scattered across the country, from the East Coast to the West and, his voice fading, named some of the missing and wanted henchmen still left.

Coughing, he smiled up at Zeke. "That ought to do it."

He closed his eyes, but Zeke shook him gently. "Jake, I've got help on the way. Don't go to sleep on me."

He looked down, trying to decide what to do to save his brother. Taking off his lightweight jacket, he held it tightly to Jake's stomach and tried to staunch the bleeding. Then he checked Jake's pulse.

Barely there. But he did open his eyes again.

Zeke held on to him, willing him to live. "Why'd you turn, Jake? You had it all. Why did you let this happen?"

Tears rolled down Jake's face. "Got caught up in the power and the money and…too late to get out. I had a price on my head, either way." He swallowed and held on to Zeke's shirt. "And so did my son."

Zeke nodded. "We'll get you help. Hang on. They're coming."

"Nah," Jake said, patting Zeke's arm. "I'm done for. Kevin?"

Penny heard him and stepped forward, her horrified gaze clashing with Zeke's. Holding Kevin close as she tried to shield him from noticing the blood flowing through Jake's dark shirt, she murmured, "Kevin is safe, Jake. He's right here."

Zeke wanted to jump up and hold her tight but…these last few minutes with Jake had to count for something. He silently offered his brother forgiveness and hoped Jake would ask the Lord the same thing. When he looked up at Penny, Zeke wondered if she'd ever forgive either of them.

Had he lost her, too?

Jake lifted his head, his gaze jumping here and there until he saw Penny and Kevin standing nearby. "Tell him, Penny. Tell him I loved him."

"He knows," she said, her distraught gaze moving from Zeke to Jake. "He'll always know that, I promise."

"Sorry I hurt you. Everything went wrong. Story of my life."

"You did the right thing tonight," she said, tears streaming down her face.

Zeke nodded. "Kevin is safe now, Jake."

Jake gave a thumbs-up sign, his eyes on his son. Then he died in Zeke's arms.

It was over at last.

Zeke held his brother, Cheetah by his side, even after the first responders showed up on the scene. He wished things could have ended differently. He thought of the good memories and he found it hard to let go.

The paramedics told him Penny and Kevin were both fine but all he could do was stare at them from a distance. Max came by and kneeled on the ground beside him, asking him questions in a firm but gentle tone. Zeke asked him about Cheetah—he'd been shot. Max had one of the paramedics examine the dog, and they deemed the courageous canine as fine. Just a flesh wound.

"Zeke, we need to check on you, man. And we need to remove Jake's body."

Zeke didn't move. The other agents all tried to talk to him but gave up and went about the work of documenting the scene and taking statements.

Finally, a hand touched his arm.

Penny. In the pale moonlight, she looked windblown and tragic, deep grief and fatigue washing her features in despair.

"Zeke, you need to let someone look at your head."

Zeke stared up at her and saw the tears in her eyes, but he was too numb and full of agony to care about himself right now. But he cared about her. He'd done everything he could to save her and his nephew. He only wished he could have saved Jake, too. He didn't know how he could ever face Kevin again, knowing how the toddler had witnessed all of this violence. Knowing he hadn't really protected any of them, after all.

"Zeke, please? You have to let him go now, okay?"

He heard the catch in Penny's words but he couldn't speak to her, couldn't tell her that he'd fallen in love with her. It was too much, too raw and messy after the tragedy of this night. He had to absorb all of this and try to find some peace and forgiveness before he could think about a future with her and Kevin.

"Go take care of your son," he said. "I'll find you later." Watching her walk away, her head down, her heart crushed, Zeke knew he loved her. But did he love her for all the right reasons?

Or did he now feel an obligation to make things right for all of them, including Jake?

An hour later—after he'd watched them take Jake's body, zipped in a dark bag, away on a stretcher—Zeke hurried to find Penny and Kevin. He only hoped to hold them both close one more time before he left the scene with Cheetah.

But Penny and her little boy weren't anywhere to be found. They were gone.

SEVENTEEN

A few weeks later, the whole team sat inside the conference room at headquarters in Billings, watching the highlights of the courtroom proceedings on the evening news. Several of them had been in the courtroom to give official reports and testimonies, Zeke included. But seeing it again now, it all seemed like a nightmare that still looped inside his head.

After the reporter signed off, Max got up and turned off the television.

"The Dupree crime family is no more," he said, a touch of grief mixed with obvious relief. Then he went on to give an updated report on the phone call he had with Zeke the night Jake died.

But Zeke knew it all. Had gone over and over it in his mind. The others knew most of it but today's debriefing would put an end to any speculation once and for all. Even though

Zara had been cleared, Max wanted her reputation intact and all rumors squelched.

Jake had a previous fling with in-going trainee Brandy Ridgeway, who at the time had been a rookie police officer he'd met in Colorado, and he'd been in touch with her almost the whole time he'd been undercover. He knew she was interested in becoming an FBI agent so he convinced her she should do it, and he'd even given her some pointers on how to prepare. But he'd cautioned her not to mention his name since he was so deep undercover. He'd also told her he'd keep in touch, just in case. Then he'd taken off with Dupree.

Brandy had passed the initial exams for training and was accepted. She didn't see Jake for months but she was in love with him, so when he contacted her for help and convinced her that he'd been set up, she told him she'd do anything he needed. He told her to get close to Zara and he got a message to her that she should watch instructor Rebecca Carwell closely.

He fooled Brandy into thinking *Rebecca* was the one stirring up trouble. So Brandy, jealous that Rebecca and Jake had once been close, goaded Zara into going to the park with her that night. Jake had hoped to talk Rebecca into helping him but she refused and didn't turn him in, thus causing an investigation to focus on her. Angry at Rebecca, he'd coerced Brandy to get the goods on her. So they launched an all-out attack on Rebecca's NATs, targeting Zara since she was so close to the K-9 team.

Nina Atkins let out a sigh. "So Agent Carwell got to the bottom of all of this without reporting it to anyone."

"Yes, but Zara knew. She had to pretend to go along with it. A kind of trial by fire," Max replied. "Rebecca followed the evidence and at first thought Zara and Brandy were both out to get her fired. So she started pushing them, hoping to make one of them crack. Apparently Rebecca figured things out pretty quickly, but she made the decision to stay quiet until she had more proof. She enlisted, or rather forced, Zara to be her eyes and ears. She was afraid Zara would report they'd seen her with a man who looked like Jake."

Dylan, who'd been listening quietly, added, "Once she realized Brandy was lying to everyone, she really needed Zara's help anyway." He looked grateful but he was still worried about Zara getting home in time for their wedding.

Max shot Dylan a grim stare. "Why don't you explain that part?"

Dylan stood. "The truth is—Brandy Ridgeway was the one who tried to sabotage the trainees, hoping to make Zara look bad. When things got too heated, Brandy panicked and deliberately failed out. Since then she'd been waiting in Colorado for Jake to come and take her out of the country. Which, by the way, he never intended to do since she failed him."

Dylan pushed at his glasses. "Meantime, Rebecca was afraid Jake would send someone to possibly harm Zara, so she gave the NATs what they thought was a false situation to solve and put *all* of them in a safe house—off-site. Only Zara knew the truth."

"Rebecca should have reported this." Nina said, anger in her words. "She should step down."

"She will step down," Max replied. "She was caught between hiding her relationship with Jake and knowing he'd betrayed her yet again and this time with one of her own trainees. She knows she used bad judgment but she did everything she could to protect Zara."

Zeke stared down at the table, a heated rage burning inside him. Jake hadn't even cared about Brandy or any of the women he'd used, nor had he cared much about Penny and Kevin, either. The battle to forgive his brother still raged in Zeke's soul. He thought he'd done so, but sitting here now, Zeke felt the same old conflicted rage.

Max continued. "Rebecca couldn't find enough on Brandy to confront her, so she kept tabs on Brandy after she left the program. When I showed up to speak to Rebecca, she knew it was all over. Rebecca sent agents to Brandy's location, hoping to get to her before we did. But we beat her there. Of course, Brandy lied to our agents and reported back to Jake immediately."

When he heard grumbles, he held up his hand. "Yes, Rebecca should have alerted us the night she met Jake in that park. Her actions after that proved she was in a panic. She made the wrong call, but in the end, she cooperated with us."

Zeke wondered if Penny knew any of this. He'd wanted to tell her but she wasn't talking to anyone these days, especially him.

The FBI had taken Brandy into custody. She'd confessed everything and told them Jake was on his way to a cabin to get Kevin. Jake had remembered hiding a witness in the safe cabin years ago. He checked it out and discovered they were there. He'd told Brandy about the cabin and how he was going to get his son, finally. But she didn't know where the cabin was located.

"Why did he do all of this with Quantico?"

Leo asked now, shaking his head. He glanced at Zeke, but Zeke didn't respond.

Max's unreadable gaze hit on Zeke, but he went on. "Jake's motivation surely stemmed from a strong need to make the FBI Classified K-9 Unit look incompetent. And it worked at times. He tracked Penny and Kevin right under our noses, kept a young recruit in his pocket and ruined her chance at becoming an FBI agent. He also tried to sabotage Zara's time in training and managed to get a senior instructor to put her career on the line for him."

Zeke couldn't take it anymore. He slammed a hand on the table. "He's dead now, and the Duprees are done. Case closed."

Max stared at Zeke for a long moment. "I'm sorry for your loss, Zeke. But…your brother took a wrong turn and we *all* lost him. Long ago, we lost him. It happens to the best of agents. And you need to remember he was one of the best before all of this took place. We know in the end, Jake proved to be a hero. He saved his little boy's life and he gave us the information we needed to finally finish off the Duprees."

The other team members gave Zeke encouraging, sympathetic glances. He remembered when he'd first walked into this place. They hadn't trusted him but they'd accepted him. Now Leo Gallagher, Julianne Martinez, Harper Prentiss, Timothy Ramsey and Nina Atkins all considered him as one of them. And the other team members had consoled him, telling him he'd done the best he could.

Max West had stood by him when he'd taken Jake's body back to Utah for burial, just Zeke, the SAC and Zeke's mother there to watch them put Jake in the ground. And a lone figure Zeke had noticed standing near a tree by the drive into the cemetery.

His father? He'd never know and he didn't care.

Earlier today, Max had offered Zeke a permanent position with the K-9 Unit. "We need people like you. You care not only about our work here, but you have good instincts and a strong sense of justice. You have a heart, Zeke. Don't forget that and don't go all cold and numb on me. I'd like you to stay and help us heal from this. We need to get back on track and get back out there doing our jobs."

"I'll think about it, Max," Zeke had responded numbly. "I just need a few days."

"Take as long as you need. I'm not going anywhere soon," Max had replied. Referring to the woman he'd met and married after investigating several bombings in California, he added, "Katerina and I have plans of our own.

I think it involves horses and…maybe a house full of children."

Zeke wanted plans, too. Plans for a future with Penny and Kevin. He could see that now that he'd had time to step back. But had he waited too long?

Penny might make good on her need to get away from Montana forever. He might have already lost her.

Penny served Rex and the one other boarder, a businessman just passing through, their noon meals, her smile as fake as the burgundy silk mums Claire had arranged in the center of the antique dining table.

"Why don't you have lunch with us?" Rex asked, ever the gentleman. "You worked hard all morning making this chicken potpie. Should eat some of it, too. Claire's joining us."

Rex had come here to go hiking and fishing for a week. But he'd apparently stayed here with Claire the whole time Penny and Kevin had been on the run and he was still here, two weeks later. Penny couldn't help but notice that those two seemed mighty chummy.

More power to them, she thought. Smiling at Rex, she said, "I nibbled while I was cooking. I'm not hungry."

Claire came ambling by, a sweet scent wafting around her. "You look like skin and bones to me, honey. We'd love to have you share a meal with us."

Claire had dressed in a pretty floral blouse and black pants. Not her usual sweatpants and baggy sweaters. Love was definitely in the air around here.

"I'm fine, Claire," Penny said. "I'm going to take some of this up to Kevin once it's cooled down a bit. I'll finish what he doesn't eat."

"I love that little boy," Rex said, winking at Claire.

Love. She felt that love and she loved both of them for watching after her and pampering her and Kevin.

But just thinking the word hurt Penny's heart so much she had to hurry back into the kitchen before she burst into tears. She cried a lot these days. For Kevin, for Jake. For Zeke...

She'd lost him the minute Jake had died. She'd seen it there in his eyes. She and Kevin would always remind Zeke of his brother. The brother he'd tried so hard to save instead of kill.

But... Jake had dived in front of Kevin to save him from Gunther's bullets. Not Zeke's. Zeke never got in a shot.

She still remembered that awful night. Woke up in cold sweats after having shadowy nightmares. She'd killed a man and in front of her little boy, at that. But how could she ever explain the terror that had captured her heart that night?

If Jake hadn't let her go and thrown himself in front of Kevin—

Her son's voice on the monitor caused Penny to race out of the kitchen and up the stairs. No matter that Claire had installed an alarm system and bought a more powerful shotgun. No matter that even now, Penny knew the FBI had people watching out for her until the trial was over and done. She'd seen them cruising by at least four times a day. No matter that Zeke had left messages and had come by to try and talk to her several times in the last few days.

None of it mattered. She couldn't face Zeke yet. She just wanted her son safe.

The minister had told her she'd be okay. That grief took many forms and came at the most unexpected times.

"I don't know why I'm grieving," she'd blurted. "Jake betrayed all of us."

"You grieve for what could have been," the kind older pastor had told her. "You grieve for what you've lost." Then he'd motioned to where Kevin sat playing with some of the new toys people had brought him after the news reports started coming in. "But Penny, you still have one thing to bring you joy and not grief. You have your son."

"I have my son," she'd echoed, smiling for the first time since this nightmare had ended.

Penny tried very hard to focus on that. So now, she swooped up her toddler and snuggled him close. "Hey, baby. Did you have a good nap?"

Kevin grinned and nodded. "Horsey?"

Penny offered him one of the other stuffed animals people had given him. "How about Giraffe?"

Kevin took it and threw it across the room. "Horsey?"

"Horsey isn't here, baby." She wouldn't cry. She couldn't. It might upset Kevin too much.

So she distracted him with the promise of outside.

They both loved outside, after all. If she could ever actually leave this yard again. She'd have to get over that phobia if she wanted to go back to work.

EIGHTEEN

After Max's reminder that they'd all lost Jake, Zeke swallowed the lump that seemed to be permanently lodged in his throat. "Thank you, sir."

It had been weeks since Jake had died in his arms. Esme Dupree had testified against Reginald Dupree, telling the jury that she'd witnessed her brother committing a murder. Her sister, Violetta, her brown-gold hair and dark cat eyes giving her an exotic flare, had been there with her, her own grief obvious in the way she held her head high and refused to wipe at the tears everyone saw in her eyes. Her brother was going to jail for life. She'd shot and killed her uncle to save Esme and now Gunther Caprice, the man she'd once loved, was dead. Violetta had verified a lot of things for them, yet again proving she had a love/hate relationship with her powerful family. But after the trial, she'd hugged Esme close and stood by her when the press had asked questions.

"My sister and I just want some peace and quiet," she'd proclaimed. "We are free now and we want to live in privacy. We can both make our own way without the help of blood money."

Esme's husband, team member Ian Slade, had also been by her side. Now that the trial was over and they'd been able to come out of the witness protection program, they planned to hold a wedding reception to celebrate.

Reginald's life sentence would ensure that he'd die behind bars and the knowledge of that at least brought the sense of justice Zeke craved. The Dupree organization had been entrenched in every type of crime from drug running to human trafficking, prostitution and gun smuggling, bribery, racketeering and murder. Sickening. But Jake's final tips had panned out in a big way. They'd raided warehouses and homes and found laptops and flash drives that told the tales of excess and greed and exposed the Dupree criminal activities across the globe.

The carnage had brought down his brother. Jake had been a good FBI agent because he needed an outlet for his rage and pain, but that same rage and pain had also caused him to covet money and power, two things he'd never had growing up.

A tragedy all the way around.

After glancing around the room, Zeke closed his eyes to *his* pain. Jake was dead, and Penny was still grieving. He'd tried to see her and console her once she was back at the Wild Iris, but she only wanted some time with her son.

"She stays up there with him mostly all day," Claire had said, shaking her head after Penny had refused to come downstairs the last time he'd come by. "They walk out in the back garden and she pushes Kevin on the tree swing but honestly, I don't think she's ready to venture past the yard yet."

Zeke understood that feeling. "Kevin will need some therapy. I know people at church who can help both of them."

"She's already had someone come by to see Kevin and she's visited with our minister, too," Claire assured Zeke. "You know how kids are. They bounce back."

But not all kids. Jake hadn't bounced back. Now Zeke wondered if he ever would, either.

After they'd been dismissed but were still milling around inside the big briefing room, Dylan came up to him. "Hey, man, thanks for forcing us to take a closer look at Zara's situation. We haven't been able to talk much but she did get one message to me. She needs me to pick up her wedding dress but I can't peek at it. She promised me she'd be here for our wedding this weekend."

"That's good," Zeke replied as they walked toward the lobby. "I wish you both the best."

Dylan stopped him with a hand on his arm. "We want you there, Zeke. At our wedding. I'm counting on you. Don't let all of this with Jake ruin things for you, man."

Then Dylan motioned for Max. He and the entire team gathered around Zeke. Getting antsy, he glared at them. "Is this some kind of intervention?"

Max held out a stuffed animal. "Yeah, I guess you could call it that. We… The team… uh…had this made for Kevin. We tried to get it as close to Cheetah as we could. You know, because the boy loves Cheetah."

Zeke took the fluffy black-and-white-spotted dog, his hand gripping the soft fur, his eyes getting misty. "This does look like Cheetah."

Dylan pushed at his glasses. "We thought this might kind of help you when you go and talk to Penny. You know?"

Leo folded his arms over his chest. "We're trying to give you an in, man. Don't blow it."

Zeke hadn't shed any tears since the night Jake died, but now he gritted his teeth against the gut-wrenching need to bawl like a baby. He could only manage a rapid nod and held tight to the stuffed animal.

Everyone dispersed just as rapidly as he stood nodding and swallowing around the lump in his throat. None of them were very good at emotions.

"So…you will show up at the church, right?" Dylan asked.

Zeke slapped a hand on Dylan's back and regained his senses. "I wouldn't miss the wedding, buddy. It'll be good to celebrate with you."

He'd be there. But first, he had to go and convince the woman he loved that they needed to be together.

Kevin ate a good bit of the chicken potpie. Penny cleaned him up and took him down the backstairs off the wraparound second-story porch. He took off running for the play area where swings and climbing equipment worked perfectly for toddler-sized adventures.

Penny sat down on a bench and laughed and clapped at his antics. He really did seem unfazed by all that had happened to him. She owed part of that to Zeke. He'd tried hard to keep Kevin occupied and distracted while they were hiding out.

She missed him so much. Too much. True,

he had tried to reach out to her, but she figured it was only to tell her goodbye before he headed back to Utah.

Deep in thought about what might have been between them, she realized her minister was right. She was grieving so many things. And losing Zeke was the main one.

"'Eke!"

Penny's head shot up at her son's joyful exclamation.

"Mommy, 'Eke!" Kevin pointed behind her, his smile melting her heart. He'd probably seen a black SUV go by on the road and thought Zeke was coming to see them.

"Hi."

Pivoting up and off the bench, she saw the man himself standing there, his heart showing in his dark eyes.

"Hi." Her pulse leaped so hard, she had to take a deep breath. In spite of the cool day, Penny's hands turned clammy.

Kevin ran up to him. "'Eke! Cheety?"

"Cheetah is resting back at headquarters," Zeke said before he scooped up the little boy into his arms. "But, hey, buddy, I brought you something."

Penny watched as he showed Kevin the medium-sized stuffed animal he'd been holding with one hand behind his back. "It's a K-9 dog that looks like Cheetah. The gang at head-quarters had it specially made just for you."

Kevin giggled and grabbed for the toy. "Cheety!"

"Cheety," Zeke said, his gaze moving from Kevin to Penny. Dropping Kevin to his feet, he smiled while Kevin ran around with the new stuffed animal, barking the way he'd heard Cheetah bark.

Tears pricked at Penny's eyes. "That's…so nice, so kind."

Zeke stood a few feet away, but the scent of spicy soap wafted in the air. He wore a black T-shirt and worn jeans and a black leather jacket. Why did he have to look so wonderful?

"You look good," he said, his eyes sliding over her face.

"I look awful and you know it," she replied, wishing she'd bothered to comb her hair and put on some makeup. Had she even put on clean jeans this morning? Yes, thankfully. And a lightweight blue sweater, too.

"Okay, so you've lost some weight. How about you and Kevin come with me? I have something I need to do and I can't do it alone."

Penny wanted to run straight into his arms but…she had to be sure. "Just like that? You come and want me to take off with you?"

Zeke moved closer. "Yes, Penny, just like

that. After too many sleepless nights and worrying myself sick with regret and guilt and grief. Just like that, I want you in my life and I want Kevin in my life. But… I can't have Jake there with us."

She gasped and put a hand to her mouth. "You still don't believe me when I say I don't love him anymore. I didn't love him when I met you, Zeke. And everything I've heard on the news in bits and pieces about him and how he used those other women made me see that I was right to run from him."

He was now only inches away. "Are you sure? Because you've refused to see me for over two weeks now."

"I've been sure for a long time. I didn't want to see you because I was afraid I'd lost you. The night he died—"

"I was a wreck," Zeke replied. "I needed some time, too. But…today after Max summed it all up, I realized I need you more than I need anything else."

Penny checked on Kevin and let out a sigh she'd been holding for weeks now. "I thought you didn't want us, Zeke. It was awful, watching you there with Jake. You went cold and dark on me. I couldn't reach you."

He pulled her into his arms and rubbed his nose against her hair. "I've wasted too much time, Penny. I can't deny how I feel about you. I just want to give it a chance. You and me and Kevin. I need both of you in my life. I want that. No more wasted time, no more regrets. We'll make our way, together."

Penny held him there, savoring his strength. She'd never felt so safe in her life. "I want that, too. Just the three of us. We can heal together."

"I like that idea," Zeke said, his hands sifting through her hair. "I need you." Then he kissed her, showing her in a tender moment that he was the real deal. Solid. Warm. Loving. True. All the things she'd been searching for.

Penny pulled away and touched her fingers to his dark bangs. Then she looked up at him and smiled. "Where are we going?"

Zeke couldn't believe she wanted to go with him. "I'm supposed to find a shelter puppy that we can train to be a future K-9 officer dog. It became a tradition…when Jake went missing. After we discovered he'd turned, the team decided to keep doing it anyway, to strengthen the unit and to honor those who've died in the line of duty, both human and canine."

He stopped once they reached the back steps of the house. "But now I'm not so sure. I said I didn't want Jake between us. Maybe we should go to a park or something. I just want to be with you and Kevin. Let's focus on that instead. I don't need to get a puppy."

"Wait," Penny said. "Zeke, I love you. Kevin loves you. There is no one here between us. We'll never forget Jake but if we're going to make this work, we have to face the tough times together. Getting a puppy will make Kevin happy and I love animals, too. We can do this one special thing, our first time together without having to look over our shoulders. Jake is gone now. We're here with you."

"Cheety," Kevin said, grinning at the stuffed dog he refused to let go of. "Woof, woof! I like puppies."

Zeke looked from the boy to Penny, his heart tripping over itself. "You do realize you just told me you love me, right?"

"Wuv," Kevin mimicked with a giggle.

"Yes," Penny said, a tentative question in her eyes. "But…how do you feel about that?"

"I love you," Zeke said before he lost his courage. "Both of you. So much."

Penny cradled his jaw in her hand. "Then let's go find a puppy. And when that dog is trained and ready to do his job, you can be proud and remember that the day we found it was also the day we found each other, okay?"

Zeke nodded, unable to speak. They headed

inside and told Claire and Rex where they were going.

Claire beamed and clapped her hands together. "And?"

"And what?" Penny said with a smile.

"And if you two are getting hitched, I want to have the wedding here, out in the garden. I'll cater it and you don't have to worry about a thing. My gift to you."

Penny blushed, her skin as fresh as peaches. "Uh… I'm not so sure…"

"We'll accept that offer," Zeke said, giving Penny a grin. "That is, if Penny *is* willing to be my wife."

The big dining room became silent. Only the ticking of the old grandfather clock sounded off the seconds.

"Wuv," Kevin said, showing Claire his miniature Cheety.

"Love," Penny echoed, tears in her eyes. "I'm willing. So willing."

Claire squealed and caught Kevin up in her arms, causing the toddler to giggle even more. Rex wiped at his eyes. And Zeke grabbed Penny close and kissed her.

"Now, go find a puppy," Claire said, her smile beaming.

They hopped into Penny's Jeep, Kevin safe in his car seat, and headed toward the local shelter. But they only made it about a mile down the road when Kevin kicked at the seat and shouted, "Puppies."

Zeke saw them, too. A little boy who looked to be about ten or so was standing by a big oak tree next to the road. A handwritten sign printed on cardboard said Puppies—One Dollar Each.

Penny gave Zeke an imploring glance. "Let's stop here."

They got out and Penny held Kevin's hand to keep him from running toward the box of yelping dogs. "Hold on. We'll see what we have."

Zeke looked at the dark-haired boy selling the puppies. He reminded Zeke of Jake, but this boy had tears in his eyes.

"I gotta sell 'em," he explained. "We're moving into Billings for my dad's new job and I can only take Muffin cause we're renting a smaller house. Muffin is their mom." He hurried on, smelling a deal. "They're part Chocolate Lab and part...we don't know. But they're good little puppies. Want one?"

Zeke picked up the runt of the litter, his heart pounding with the sure knowledge that God was always in the details. The brown-colored puppy licked at his hands and face. "I'll take all four," he said. "I hope they can be trained to possibly become K-9 dogs."

"Those are good dogs," the boy said, smiling for the first time. "They save lives and catch bad guys."

"Yes, they do," Penny said, her gaze holding Zeke's.

"Listen," Zeke said, kneeling with Kevin by the box. "I'm gonna give you one hundred dollars, but only if you promise to come and visit these puppies at the training center in Billings." He handed the boy five twenties and gave him a business card with all the information. "And I also need to speak to your parents."

The boy bobbed his head and took the money and the card up to where two people sat on the porch steps, watching.

"Why do you need to speak to them?" Penny asked, glancing up toward the house.

"Look around," Zeke replied, awe in the words.

Penny glanced at the house and the yard. "Zeke…"

"A house with a picket fence and a nice yard, Penny," he said. "And I'm guessing there might be a stream in the back. If not, we'll make do with the house and this amazing view."

The boy's parents came down and thanked Zeke for his generosity. "You've done us a big favor," the dad said. "He's been fretting about these puppies since they were born."

Zeke smiled and explained the training program. "I hope you'll come and visit, take a tour." Then he gave Penny a hopeful smile. "And I was wondering... I don't see a for-sale sign. Do you rent this place?"

The man shook his head. "No. We just talked to a Realtor last week about putting it on the market. I have to be in Billings in about a month or so. Are you interested?"

Zeke gave Penny another expectant glance. "Are you ready?" he asked her.

"We could look," she replied, tears in her eyes.

"It's a nice piece of property," the woman said. "There's a quiet little stream out back."

Zeke smiled at Penny. She smiled back. "We'd appreciate a tour, if not today then whenever we can arrange it."

"C'mon in," the boy's mother said. "I just cleaned it up for the Realtor anyway."

Leaving the boy to guard the puppies, Zeke lifted Kevin into his arms and they all went up to the white farmhouse-style home with the big, deep front porch.

He held Kevin close and took Penny by the hand. "Are you sure about this?" he asked, still in awe.

"Very sure," she said, her beautiful eyes

filled with hope and love. "You're going to make a great daddy, Zeke."

Kevin bobbed his head, not really understanding but picking up on the words anyway. "'Eke." He pointed to the man holding him. "Daddy."

EPILOGUE

"Is she here yet?"

Penny turned to the worried groom standing in the church hallway behind her. "No. I promised the bridesmaids I'd let them know the minute Zara gets here, but… Zeke got word that she's on her way from the airport. ETA is any minute now." Then she pushed Dylan back. "And you can't see her before the wedding, so go get ready to take your place at the altar."

Dylan's blue eyes were bright with hope. "Is my tie straight?"

Penny glanced over his dark suit and crisp white shirt. He wore a blue tie that matched his eyes. "Your tie is perfect. Stop being so nervous."

Dylan nodded and took off to the front of the church. Penny had been given the task of scouting for Zara. After hearing what had happened at Quantico, she couldn't wait to meet the newly minted FBI agent. Zara's experience had been harrowing, so Penny felt a bond with her already. And wished for the hundredth time that they could have all saved Jake.

"Hey."

She whirled around to find Zeke standing there, smiling at her. "You make the cutest lookout." His eyes moved over her flowing burgundy dress. "I don't think I've ever seen you in a dress before. I like it."

"You told me that already," she said through a grin. "Several times." She patted her upswept hair. "And Claire did me up nice."

"She sure did," Zeke said, giving her a gentle kiss.

The last week had been amazing. Claire had offered her a job as manager of the Wild Iris. "So Rex and I can take that trip across the country I've always dreamed about."

Those two were getting married at Christmas.

And Zeke and Penny had agreed on a Valentine's Day wedding, after Claire and Rex returned from their honeymoon.

"One good thing came out of this," Zeke said as he stood there with her, his dark suit fitting his broad shoulders to perfection. "We all found someone to spend the rest of our lives with."

Penny laughed. "So Max is married to Katerina and they have two dogs and two training puppies and lots of horses."

He nudged her hair with his nose. "Yes. And Leo and Alicia are married. They got married a few months ago."

"Okay, then we have Riley and Harper. Harper and I talked about her wedding plans."

"Yes, they're engaged. Riley's mother moved in with him to help with his nephew, Asher, but Asher is much better now." Zeke had told her about Asher's mother being murdered and Asher being severely injured. Riley and Harper took down the killer.

"Then Julianne and Brody are planning to get married here in Montana, before he heads off to Quantico this spring."

"You're getting good at this," Zeke said, his lips touching on her neck. "They're training two pups, Cooper and Hawk."

Penny enjoyed being near him but slapped at his shoulder. "And Ian and Esme will renew their vows next week."

Zeke tugged her close. "Yep. You're all caught up, except for one couple." He grinned and touched his forehead to hers.

"Us," she said. "We're buying a house, I have a new job and we're getting married on Valentine's Day." She laughed. "And we're training two very active Chocolate Lab–mix puppies."

"You *are* good at this." He kissed her again. Penny closed her eyes and almost pinched herself.

But when she opened her eyes, she spotted a taxi and pulled away with a squeal. "Get lost. The bride is here!"

Zeke watched as Zara rushed up the aisle to her waiting groom, her full white skirt swishing. Dylan left the altar and met her halfway up the aisle and lifted her into his arms while the organist tried to keep up.

"You made it," Dylan said, tears in his eyes.

"I'm here." Zara's dark hair was caught up in a careless ponytail and she had one bright white flower tucked into the band holding her curls. But her smile said it all. "I'm ready to get married."

Everyone in the church clapped with happiness. Zeke turned to Penny and took her hand in his. Together, they watched their friends say their wedding vows.

An hour later, the whole team and all the people who worked behind the scenes with Dylan, various friends and family, and Claire and Rex, who'd brought Kevin to see everyone, gathered out behind the church where tents and tables had been set up in a beautiful fall motif and a huge cake from Petrov's Bakery stood in three tiers decorated with burgundy and green edible flowers. Zeke's heart, once so cold and numb, now held hope and the beautiful promise of having a true family at last.

"I love you," he whispered to Penny as they danced to a soft waltz.

"I love you back," she said, her eyes glimmering with that same hope and promise.

Dylan and Zara took off toward the parking lot, holding hands and laughing.

"Are you leaving?" Zeke called.

"No. We have a surprise for everyone," Dylan called out.

In the next few minutes, several handlers unleashed a pack of trained K-9 dogs and several still-in-training puppies that soon overtook the dance floor.

Every K-9 partner was there, including Cheetah. The curious canine hurried when Zeke called him and was soon dancing with them while the puppies flipped and flopped over each other and everyone else. A lot of laughing and yelping ensued.

"Chaos," Max said as he whirled by with Katerina. "And I wouldn't have it any other way."

"Me, either," Zeke replied. "For once, we're all here and accounted for."

"And we're happy," Penny said, laughing.

He looked into the big-sky sunset and then he looked back at the woman he loved. "Happy…and blessed."

* * * * *

*If you enjoyed TRACKER by Lenora Worth,
look for the other books in the
CLASSIFIED K-9 UNIT miniseries:*

*GUARDIAN by Terri Reed
SHERIFF by Laura Scott
SPECIAL AGENT by Valerie Hansen
BOUNTY HUNTER by Lynette Eason
BODYGUARD by Shirlee McCoy
CLASSIFIED K-9 UNIT CHRISTMAS
by Terri Reed and Lenora Worth*

Dear Reader,

I hope this story kept you on the edge of your seat. It sure kept me that way when I was writing it. My heart hurt for Zeke and Penny. Forced together by tragedy and danger, they found hope and a way around all the obstacles in their way. It was painful to put a child in such a situation but sadly, we know this can sometimes happen, so little Kevin now has a good home with a wonderful man to be his daddy!

I hope this story enlightened and entertained you. If you've ever had bad times in your life, know that God is there and He watches over all of us. He certainly guided me through this story.

Until next time, may the angels watch over you. Always.

Lenora Worth

Get 2 Free Books,
Plus 2 Free Gifts—
just for trying the *Reader Service!*

Love Inspired

Get 2 Free Books,
Plus 2 Free Gifts —
just for trying the
Reader Service!

HARLEQUIN

HEARTWARMING™

HWI7R